**BOYS**

# Jeremy Aldana

Annabella,

Dream Big; Shoot For The Stars! Never
Give Up, Never Give In, And Never
Stop Believing...

Create Lasting Memories, Enjoy
All that Life Has To Offer, And
Grab Ahold Of The Opportunities
That Come Your Way...

Trust Your Instincts, Recognize
Your Worth, And Never Forget What's
In Your Heart...

# Prologue
## July 17th, 1990

"We now go live to Greenfield Avenue, where Bill Michelson is reporting on a tragic event that has just taken place."

"Thank you Gretchen, I'm at the intersection of 86th and Greenfield Avenue, where a terrible accident has turned this normally upbeat neighborhood into a somber gathering place. The residents here, as you can see, are huddling next to each other, not quite believing what has happened.

"Just behind me, across the street, there was a terrible accident. A deadly collision occurred when one vehicle crossed the centerline and collided, head on, with another.

"It was just a little over an hour ago when the accident occurred. The authorities are reporting that there are no survivors. The victims' names are being withheld at this time, until their families can be contacted.

"Authorities have told us that the occupants of one of the vehicles, a station wagon, were a young woman and two children. A few residents here, who knew this young family, have told me that one of the children was not in the vehicle at the time of the crash. Some have now left the immediate area and have begun to search for the remaining child, a young boy."

"Thank you Bill, is there anything you can tell us about the driver?"

"Yes, Gretchen, the authorities are telling me that the driver, who crossed the centerline and caused the accident, was fleeing from arrest after he was pulled over a few miles back for suspicion of driving under the influence.

"The authorities are still taking statements from witnesses at this time, and I will be checking back in with more details as they unfold. This is Bill Michelson reporting live, for TMJ4."

"Thank you Bill, our prayers go out to this young family and their loved ones, on this tragic day."

# BOYS WILL BE BOYS

## Dr. Ron
## Summer 1990

My name is Joey, and I wanted it stated for the record (whatever the record actually is) that I am writing this under protest. Dr. Ron says that I have to at least try, and my aunt and uncle say that I have to go to see him every week, so you can see how I'm kinda stuck. He says that I never have to show this to anyone, not even him, and I guess that's cool, but then why do I have to write it at all?

I feel like I'm writing a diary, like a girl would. Yes, I really do feel that way, even though he says that boys can call theirs journals. On top of the diary thing, writing this makes me feel like I'm doing some kind of homework assignment. He says that when I write in this thing, it's like doing homework for my soul, whatever he means by that. See my point, soul or no soul, it's still homework!

He says that every time I sit down to write in this thing, that I should put a date on the top of each entry (see, only diaries use the word entry!), on account (he says) that

when I'm older and looking back, it will make each entry

more specific in my mind. He tried explaining something

about my memories and how dates attached to them

sometimes will make them more vivid, and will allow me to

remember more details.

He told me that most good writers don't use

flashbacks when they write, but since I was writing a journal,

they would be okay for me. He said that writing flashbacks

meant that I was writing the memory, from my head, the way

that I remembered it at the time it actually happened. He said

that it would help me organize my thoughts and give my

emotions a place to be expressed. He said that my family

would always be in my memories, and that by writing them

down, I was giving them a place to live forever. When he put

it that way, I guess I understood a little bit better.

For me to put a date on each entry, for the purpose

of some future reading, is a bit odd to me, even though I

guess I can understand it a little. The problem is that I've

never really thought about the future in terms of something I

might do later in my life. I mean, I've thought about the

future before, but those thoughts were never personally about

me.

Sure, I always wondered if someone would ever land

on Mars or if we'd ever meet some kind of Alien in our

lifetime (but not the 'War of the Worlds' or the 'Area 51'

type). I've thought about whether the Brewers would ever

win the pennant again, or if they'd ever win '12' in a row like

they did in '87, so 'George Webb' would give us all free

burgers like last time. I've thought about the Bucks too, and if

they'd ever be able to beat those Larry Bird lead Celtics or

those 'Bad Boys' from Detroit.

I think that I might be confusing myself, with all of

this writing of my thoughts. It feels weird, like taking a

shower with all my clothes on. Dr. Ron said it might feel

weird for a while, but that it will get easier the more times I write. I'm not sure if I believe him or not, but he seems

decent enough and what do I have to lose, anyway. He says it

will help with my grieving process, which I guess is why I was

sent to see him in the first place. I guess I'll give it a shot,

even though I'm not sure if I'm doing it right.

The reason I had to see him to begin with, was cause

my aunt and uncle were concerned about me. They were

worried, on account that my family was involved in an

accident recently, and they wanted to make sure that I was

gonna be okay. I just had my 13th birthday, but I wish that I

could've stayed 12 years old for just one more day.

It was on my birthday, of all days, when my mom and

my brothers, Jacob and Bobby, were killed in a car accident. I

miss them a lot and I wish they were here right now,

especially cause if they were, than I wouldn't have to write in

this thing anymore.

# BOYS WILL BE BOYS

I haven't cried yet and I'm not sure why. I overheard my aunt and uncle talking about not seeing me cry since the accident, and I think that's why they sent me to Dr. Ron.

After I heard that, I'd rub my eyes really hard every morning, before I went upstairs, until they were red and puffy. I'd even make the last minute of my shower be cold water, so I'd have the proper sniffles. I didn't want them to worry about me, so when they showed concern for me not crying, I showed them what they needed to see. Despite the early morning crying charade, they still insisted that I go to see him every Monday afternoon, and since they were now my 'legal guardians', I had no other choice.

You know, reading what I just wrote there didn't sound that good, especially since it was my own voice, in my head, reading back to me. The deal is, I love my aunt and my uncle, and they just want what's best for me. I know somewhere in the back of their minds, their probably concerned about me committing suicide, but I'm not gonna do nothing like that. And, if they want me to see this doctor

guy, then that's what I'll do. After all, he even told me that I

only need to see him for as long as I feel I need to. I had

asked him to tell that to my aunt and uncle, which he did, and

they ended up agreeing to the arrangement. I told them that I

appreciated how they were looking out for me.

I told him about my not being able to cry, and how I

faked it for my aunt and uncle. Then I asked him a question;

something like, "What's wrong with me, Doc? How come I

ain't crying yet?"

He told me that he'd seen this kinda thing before,

where it's difficult for a person to express their emotions in

extreme situations. He also told me about all kinds of people

who had trouble crying after their loved ones died sudden

and tragically.

He said that sometimes it was a physical issue, like

they had some condition with their tear ducts, or something,

whatever they were. He also said that everyone grieves

differently; this is where he said that I fit in. He said,

sometimes kids react on extreme levels, on account of their

limited life experience, meaning we're so young that we don't

always understand what death means. He said that often, kids

still think that their loved ones are coming back somehow.

He was real cool about explaining it to me. He didn't

talk down to me, or talk to me like I was dumb or anything. I

understood that they were gone, and I am still kinda in shock,

but he says that's normal enough. I want to cry, I really do; I

even try to cry, and I hurt whenever I think about them, but

for some reason, I can't. He says that it's okay, and that it was

between me and him.

He wasn't so much like a friend or a parent, or even a

cool uncle, but was something different altogether. He was

there every week to listen and give me advice. I guess, if I had

to put it into words, I'd say he was more like a tutor for me,

which I'm okay with.

# Jeremy Aldana

My dad died just before I was born, so I never knew him. My brothers were so young that they didn't remember him at all. Mom used to tell me that I looked just like my dad, but of the pictures I saw, I couldn't really tell. I always used to think that she told me that, so I wouldn't be left out, on account that I never got to meet him. Mom used to do things like that, always trying to make it up to me, always letting me know that I mattered. She was cool like that, cause I knew some moms who didn't give half that much effort.

I don't ever plan on showing this to anyone, but I wonder what Dr. Ron would think about how I've done so far. I decided that I would put dates on the entries. I will call it a journal and that'll be enough to get started. I know that I don't want to go to any support groups or take any medication, on account that I'm not depressed. I'm sad, but with Dr. Ron and the boys, I got a good shot of surviving this, I think.

# BOYS WILL BE BOYS

I miss mom the most, and I wonder if that's fair to Jake and Bobby. I didn't tell anyone that, so I don't know if that's normal. It's weird that their not here anymore. I try to think about that, but I don't get too far before my brain shuts down and I just sit there and stare. I know when it comes on, cause my eyes get unfocused and I just sit there saying to myself, "snap out of it."

The boys have been real supportive and haven't bugged me to talk about it. They say that they're here for me, like always, and then they leave it at that. The boys were always like family before, but now they are like my only family, if that makes any sense.

I told the boys about Dr. Ron and the journal, and they were cool about it. They even suggested that they all start a journal like mine, so I didn't have to do it alone. I told them that it was cool that they wanted to do that, but that it wasn't necessary. They said that they understood, and I told them, "thanks."

11

# Jeremy Aldana

## Packers, and Broncos, and Bears, and Cowboys, Oh My!
### Fall 1990

Our neighborhood was as bright and colorful as Mighty Mouse's cape was, with flowers and gardens in almost everyone's front yards. The suburbs weren't so bad, I mean people were still people, but there was a different lifestyle for sure. If you lived in the suburbs, chances were that your parents had good jobs. Or in our case, mom just wanted us away from the gangs of the city and into a safer neighborhood. Despite her intentions, I think we would have done alright had we stayed in the city. The only thing I really missed about the city was going to Mitchell Park. It wasn't just the park or its famous Domes with their exotic plants and such, but it was 'Suicide Hill' (only the biggest and scariest sledding hill in the world) that made the park awesome. Then again, if we hadn't moved to the 'burbs', I don't think that I would have ever met any of the boys.

# BOYS WILL BE BOYS

Whether it was in the movies or in the books, the boys seemed to fit into a certain type of mold when it came to stereotyped groups. I wasn't sure if that was a good thing or not, but I guess it didn't matter anyway. There was the classic goofball, which was Paul. Jack was the troubled rebel. Mark was the little man overachiever. Andy was the brainiac. Brad was the peacemaker. And yours truly, was the leader of our group; 'The Boys'.

Every fall, up till this one, the boys, my brothers, and me had football on our brains and our bodies were our weapons. It was always cold and usually started snowing by the end of September, which of course made for perfect football weather. And of course, the extent of our scratches, bruises, and scars were our way of measuring who was the toughest.

We played the games at the high school and man was it awesome! The chalk was always bright, the field was huge, and that was about all we needed. Sundays were the best day of the week, on account that we were all pumped up from watching our teams play on TV. By Sunday afternoon, we were ready to inflict our own brand of pain on each other.

We all had our own teams that we liked the best, each one the boys. Andy's favorite player was Bo Jackson, on account that nobody messed with Bo Jackson. Nobody could push Bo around and Andy saw something in that quality. Paul liked Jerry Rice the best, probably because he was only like the best wide receiver ever to play the game of football.

Brad's favorite was Joe Montana. He and Paul would always be on the same team every Sunday, and always hooked up for the deep ball, just like their real life counterparts. Mark's favorite was a kicker named Rich Karlis who used to play with Broncos. Karlis was the toughest guy who ever kicked field goals, in the history of the NFL. We all thought he was crazy, on account that he kicked them with a bare foot, in the rain and snow and everything! I think Mark liked him the best, cause he was tough just like Karlis. He always

14

felt he had to prove to everyone just how tough he was, that's what 'little man's syndrome' does to a kid.

Jack's favorite was none other than the infamous Mike Singletary of the Bears. He was the leader of the best defense in football (maybe all-time), playing middle linebacker. He was one of the smartest players in the game and I think that's why Jack liked him so much, on account that Jack was big and smart too, even though people thought he wasn't, just cause of how big he was.

My team was the Broncos, and they were from Denver. It snowed a lot there, like it did here, and that made football on Sundays even better. I'd be John Elway, their quarterback, who could engineer the best two-minute drive in the game. He ran past defensive ends and linebackers, giving his body up for the yards, and for the team. He could throw the ball just about the whole length of the field and then on the next play, do it again.

# Jeremy Aldana

Elway wore number 7, which was my favorite number. It was my favorite, on account that I was born on July 17, 1977. It's been my favorite number for as long as I can remember. People told me it's lucky, cause it was one of God's favorite numbers too, but I didn't know much about him.

My other favorite team, besides the Broncos, was the Green Bay Packers, of course. I loved the Packers, if not for any other reason than it was required of those who lived in Wisconsin. Maybe one day the Packers and the Broncos could play against each other in the Super bowl. I can dream, can't I?

Mom used to worry about us getting our clothes dirty, playing outside, but she couldn't stop us. No way she could've; we were too crafty for that. Instead, she'd always tell us not to get too dirty. I would tell her that it's o.k. cause 'God made dirt, so dirt don't hurt'. I don't know if she ever listened to me though. I only knew that she worked real hard to get us those clothes, and that she never bought us anything white in color.

My older brother, only by like a year and a half, was Bobby and his jersey on game days was that of Walter Payton, number 34. Payton was a running back (only the best all-time) that played for the Bears, just like Mike Singletary. Bobby's real name was Robert Michael James Harris, so it was obvious why we used to call him Bobby. Despite everyone in our family, our school, and our state hating the Chicago Bears with a passion, Bobby stuck to his guns and rooted for his team every Sunday.

My oldest brother was Jake, well Jacob, and he used to be my hero. Man, I sure looked up to him. He was tall and didn't look much like Bobby and me, but we knew he was golden, at least to us anyway. He was three years older than me, so we never hung out much, which was probably why he was my hero for so long. His game day jersey was that of Tony Dorsett, number 33 of the Dallas Cowboys. This guy

# Jeremy Aldana

was different from Sir Walter who perfected the 'dive over the pile for a score'. It was Dorsett who would just plain run over a guy, if he was in the way.

Even though Payton dove for score after score, the best display of a guy giving up his body for the game was when Nat Moore caught a pass from Dan Marino on Monday Night Football, back in 1984. Moore ran a route over the middle of the field and got nailed by two New York Jets at the same time, one from each side, causing his body to spin completely around like helicopter blades. The 'Helicopter Catch' will surely go down in history as one of the best catches ever.

It was outside that all the fun happened. None of us were ever inside much, except when it got real dark. In the summer, it was different, the rules changed. 'Less Rules, Equals More Fun' or as Jake would always say, 'Maximize the pleasure, Minimize the pain'. I'm sure it meant something different for him, but I understood it well enough, in my own way.

It was after he said that to me, in one of his 'big brother talks', that me and the boys made a pact to always get our homework done either at school or right away when we got home. It was sheer genius for us at the time; do homework and get good grades, and then our parents had no choice but to let us stay out late (as long as we were together).

We were boys and we were living the 'American Dream' or so that's what Brad's dad used to say. He'd tell us that we'd never forget these times. He said that we always had to be there for each other because most likely we'd all, one day, move on with our lives and only have the memories.

We liked Brad, he was cool, but man, his dad sure was a bummer. We never wanted not to be friends. We thought we'd be together forever. And it was after one of his dad's talks that we all made another pact, this one to never lose touch with each other. We weren't stupid, we knew that after

19

high school we'd all move on to bigger and better things, but we also knew that if we stuck together then not even a freight train could move us.

Brad was the peacemaker, the one who always made sure that whatever we were doing, we were doing together. His dad always wore coveralls and red suspenders, when we saw him, which wasn't much, on account that he was a truck driver. We all kinda felt for Brad, cause we saw his dad about as much as he did.

He had a tough house, and that's why he was always the first to my house after school. I guess he didn't like being at home almost as much as his dad didn't. Whenever Brad was late for something, we'd have to go to his house and get him. He never wanted us to come in, and after the first time that we all did, we knew why he hadn't wanted us to.

20

# BOYS WILL BE BOYS

## Broken Homes
## Fall 1990

We all heard yelling, and heard Brad screaming for his

mom to stop. We were scared for him, but we knew that if

the same thing were happening to anyone of us, Brad would

be the first in to make sure we were alright. We at least owed

him that much. When we walked in the front door, Brad was

bent over and crouching on the floor. We all looked at each

other and ran over to him. He was picking up his mom's,

now shattered, glass vase. It was the one he had given her on

her birthday that past summer. Within seconds, we were right

there with him cleaning up the broken glass.

The screaming had stopped when Brad's older sister,

Mary, ran out the front door we'd left open when we came in.

Brad was wiping his face dry cause he didn't want us to see

him crying. His mom was washing her hands in the sink and I

could see, out of the corner of my eye, that the water

splashing off her hands was red.

Brad's mom had cut her hand when she smashed the vase on the kitchen counter, and it flew back up at her. It was then, that I saw Brad's hands were bloody too. It was hard to tell if he got cut though, on account that his hands were shaking so badly.

After we left Brad's that day, without him, none of us ever brought it back up to him; neither did we ever go back inside his house. It was Brad's dad never being there that caused the heartache in their house, I think.

Brad's mom always called his sister a 'pot head', whatever that was. Brad swore us all to secrecy the next day, after he told us. He told us that before that day, with all the screaming and yelling, that Mary was doing drugs. She was smoking them.

"Like cigarettes?" I remember asking him.

He said it was kind of like that, but worse. He said Mary would either hide in the bathroom with the fan on, or lock herself in her room.

# BOYS WILL BE BOYS

Brad told us that she only locked her door after he walked in on her, one day after school, while she was smoking. He told us that her eyes turned red and she was always tired after smoking. He said that she told him never to use drugs and if she ever caught him, she'd break his neck.

Mary told him that both their mom and their dad smoked pot too, so they had no right to tell her that she couldn't. Brad never talked to his parents about it, but he did believe Mary. Along with making us swear that we'd take it to the graves with us, Brad, said that Mary had been stealing the drugs from their parents and that was why they were always fighting with her.

The day of the big fight, the one we witnessed, changed Brad, cause he didn't see his sister everyday anymore. Mary left and never came back. He missed her lots, but we never talked about it much. We all felt it whenever Brad looked sad, cause it sucked that his sister ran away.

## Jeremy Aldana

We were the boys, and we were always there for each
other. When one of us would get down about something or
get into a tight jam, we'd be right beside each other every
time. And when we all couldn't be there at the same time,
we'd always make sure that someone was there. We all had
our own strengths and weaknesses. Sometimes, it felt like we
knew each other better than we knew ourselves, if that was
possible.

We could always count on Paul to make us laugh. If
there ever was a class clown, it was him. Sometimes he would
even make the teacher laugh, which made us all laugh even
harder. Lunch was the worst time to be around him, cause it
never failed that one of us would be spewing soda or milk
from our nose and mouth. It was like he waited for us to take
a big drink and then he would look right at you and once he
did, you knew it was over.

The lunchroom was Paul's playground and I used to
swear that he was gonna grow up to be a comedian one day.

24

# BOYS WILL BE BOYS

Although he never admitted it to us, I still think he waited for us to take a drink before he told his jokes.

Paul was almost the exact opposite of Brad, and I think that's why they got along so well. Paul was skinny, with 'coke-bottle' style glasses and Brad could read the serial numbers off our dollar bills from five feet away. Paul wore funky clothes that were always worn out and were always plaid and flannels. He was the youngest boy of six in his family, and as we all knew, when you were the youngest, you got the 'hand-me-downs'.

Brad had the summer job of mowing everybody in the neighborhoods' lawns, so he had money to buy his own clothes. Of course, we all wanted to help him spend it on stuff for us. We only gave him grief every now and then, cause we all knew Paul and what he had to deal with.

Paul was always happy though, hand-me-downs and everything, or so he seemed. His family was normal enough, and he was as normal as a suburban kid could be. His five

Jeremy Aldana

older brothers occupied all three schools in town: the grade school, the middle school, and the high school. His dad worked all day and his mom stayed at home. Even with five kids, all boys, their house somehow managed to stay clean most of the time.

Paul slept on the top bunk and because he was the youngest and smallest, he always had to wait to use the bathroom until everybody else in the house had their turns. I think that's why every time we'd all sleep over at each other's houses, he'd take showers that lasted for like an hour. I'd know, cause we'd always have to wait for him. We let him, though, cause we understood. Plus it was really funny when he'd get out, cause his fingers and toes looked all pruned out like a raisin. We'd joke that Hollywood was gonna call him and ask him to be the newest 'California Raisin'.

Paul never complained about being the youngest and smallest, so it was easy for us to do it for him. And we knew he kinda liked it, cause he never stopped us or defended

26

them. Dr. Ron said we were like his outlet or something, whatever that meant.

# Jeremy Aldana

## ProWings
## Winter 1990

One of my chores used to be to take the garbage out, on account that mom always said that was why she had boys, to do the 'man work'. I did dishes too; it wasn't like I was lazy or nothing, and she was pretty cool about it. I think she just always wanted to have a clean house. I could understand that too, cause it was usually me and the boys who made most of the messes. For the record, I always cleaned up before they got there and they always helped me before we left. Me and the boys still clean sometimes, and my aunt and uncle tell me they appreciate it.

My room, however, was a completely different story. I lived in the basement, which was set up like an apartment back from when Jake stayed down there. I kept my room clean, for the most part, but it wasn't like 'spotless' or anything.

# BOYS WILL BE BOYS

I'd never been one to make my bed in the morning, neither was my mom. She wasn't like some of the kids' moms at school or around the neighborhood who made their kids beds, cleaned their rooms, and made them lunches. The boys used to call her 'mom', on account that she was cooler than most moms were. She used to tell me that she liked being cool and told me that she enjoyed having the boys around all the time, which of course worked for me.

When winter was in full swing, it got real cold and that was usually when we could be found inside, usually at my house. It would get so cold that your boogers froze right inside of your nostrils when you walked outside, the grass would crunch under your feet, and you could always see your breath.

Shoveling snow wasn't too bad, I guess. I mean, I never minded it too much, cause it gave me time to just think. I also got to build up my muscles at the same time. I would even shovel the neighbors' sidewalk sometimes, even though they never once brought their snow blower over to help me out. I was never mad though, but maybe a bit bitter, cause I knew that it was better to give than to receive. Mom taught me that years ago, I remember.

Snowball fights were fun, but they sure were cold. You've got to understand, that if anyone tells you that they can make and throw a good snowball with gloves on, then they're full of 'you know what'! The powder kind was no good. No, it had to be the cold packing snow for good snowballs. And of course, it never failed that every winter there was at least one time when the snow would get wet and would make the perfect 'ice-ball'.

If you got nailed with an ice-ball, you were gonna hit the ground and there would be some bruising. For some reason, ice-balls seemed to travel, midair, upward and hit their intended target right in the face. The fun was over when one of us actually took one in the face, but we were sure to tease him about it for at least a day. We could be brutal sometimes, but we were the boys and that was the same as family.

Jack was the rebel among us, but not like that James Dean guy that was in all those old movies. I think Jack would've survived in the Bronx, wherever that was. He was a bruiser, who was, to say the least, a big kid for his age. He was at least a half a foot taller than most of us and probably weighted close to 225 pounds.

The football coach from the high school came to every one of our Sunday games at the school. The coach said that if he was gonna allow us to play on his field, then we were gonna let him watch. Jack was smart and knew that Coach Walker was scouting him for the high school team. There were probably college recruiters secretly taping our games too, but Jack didn't care.

Jack knew that he was one of the boys, even when we gave him a ration about being the muscle. I used to think, on account that he was so smart, that the rebel image never really fit him. He was a kid with a big heart who had seen enough hate, violence, and hurt to last a lifetime. He would do just about anything for the chance to argue with an adult. So, I guess in his own way, he was a rebel. We never stood in line when he was with us and he wouldn't let any adult tell us what to do, but he was still just like us.

One summer, he even wore 'ProWings', the shoes that poor kids wore cause they only cost like five dollars, and made all of us tell our parents that we wanted them too. I mentioned already how big he was, didn't I? We boycotted all the big companies, cause he read an article about these places that made kids our age make the shoes. He called them 'sweat shops' cause they would cram all those kids into a hot building with no ventilation and make them work like adults. Actually it was worse, cause adults could say no but those kids were forced to do it. We were all pissed off when we found this out, but Jack was super-pissed.

# BOYS WILL BE BOYS

He once took off on Mark and got a rude wakeup call when Mark fought back, even though Jack was like twice his size. None of us were surprised when Mark fought back, of course. It wasn't that Jack was a bully, cause he had a heart of gold, but we knew the time he spent in Juvenile Hall did a number on him. Besides that, he had no right attacking Mark, just cause Mark was defending Andy.

Jack was picking on Andy about not standing up to his parents who kept blaming him for stealing their money, when he wasn't doing it. Jack thought he was helping Andy, but he couldn't see that he was doing the same thing that his dad did to him, and when Mark called him out on it, that's when Jack took off on him. None of us knew why Jack even tried, cause he, of all people, knew that Mark could hold his own.

Mark had what Jacob, my older brother, once called 'little-man syndrome', cause when Mark started, he didn't stop. Some would say that he 'spazed out', but Mark would tell you that he was in total control and that he had something to prove. And as a result, Mark single-handedly brought Jack back down to Earth. What resulted was a hard fall and a black eye with a blood clot.

After Jack held his eye for a while, probably wishing he'd never went after Mark, he hugged both Mark and Andy. He said his apologies, and, of course, all was forgiven. After all, we were the boys and we couldn't be separated for anything.

Jack had it rough at home, just like the rest of us, maybe more so. I think that we were more of a family to him than he had at home. Just like Brad, he didn't ever invite us to his house. He was embarrassed and none of us blamed him. His sister was always in counseling, on account that his dad abused the crap of out of her. His dad abused his mom too, but made the mistake of hitting Jack once. And once was all that Jack needed, cause a year ago, Jack proceeded to put the big hurt on him.

# BOYS WILL BE BOYS

He put his prick of a dad in the hospital for two weeks after taking his favorite bat, his 'Louisville Slugger', to his dad's arms, knees, and head. Jack washed dishes at a local diner all summer to save up for that baseball bat. I guess, in a weird kind of way, it served its purpose.

# Jeremy Aldana

## Louisville Slugger
## Flashback to Winter 1989

After Jack beat his dad silly, he came running over to

my house where me and the boys were playing Tecmo Bowl

on the Nintendo. Jack was a mess. He was crying and

sweating, and his white t-shirt was red. His dad's blood was

splattered all over his jeans and his ProWings. The police

came over to the house and wanted Jack to go with them.

And, if you knew Jack, you knew that he wasn't going

without a fight (and we had his back too).

When the cops showed up, we told Jack to go into

the bathroom and decided that we wouldn't answer the door.

It probably wasn't the brightest idea we ever came up with,

on account that we should've known the cops wouldn't leave

so easily. It wouldn't have been that difficult to know where

Jack was, on account that there was a nice big blood trail

leading up to the door. If you haven't seen it before, blood stands out pretty well when it's on top of white snow. Even Mr. Magoo could've found him.

After the cops looked through the windows and saw us, they threatened to break down the door (which I'm sure the boys would've all pitched in to help replace). We then all made the decision to 'face the music', as my mom used to say. When we opened the door, one of them asked us where Jack was. We knew the question was a stall tactic, on account that we knew what his partner was doing. After all, we weren't stupid. Those cops weren't the first cops we'd ever seen, nor would they be the last.

The cops, in those days, weren't like the ones when we were younger. These ones didn't introduce themselves, they never waved to us on the street, and they stopped handing out baseball cards to us a few years before. Most kids ran the other way when they saw the cops, even if they weren't doing anything wrong. At any given point of the night you could hear a kid hollering "Five-O," which was

code for the 'the cops are on their way' or 'the cops are here'.
The code came from an old television show called "Hawaii
Five-O" about cops.

They stopped walking the neighborhoods and instead
drove slowly up and down them, stopping and harassing
anyone of us for hanging out. There were gangs around, but
we all stayed clear and didn't want anything to do with them.
But, I guess the cops in those days had problems telling the
difference between us and the gangbangers. They did crazy
stuff, like making us break up and walk separately home,
sometimes even following us all the way to our front yards.
Their excuse was that whenever they saw more than three of
us together, after six o'clock at night, then we were
considered a gang.

We knew there were bad people out there, but all they
had to do was take some time and get to know us. If they had
taken the time, then they would've never seen us as a threat.
But they never did get to know any of us, and man was it

annoying having to listen to them talk down to us like they were better and smarter than us just cause they were grown-ups.

Anyway, knowing that the lug at the front door was distracting us, we saw that his partner (who by the way should've stopped eating doughnuts when he started losing his hair) was still lurking around the yard. Neither of them were any kind of match for Jack, even though they were a good twenty years older than us. We knew that it was now or never for us to make our move, and so we let our adrenaline take over.

Remember, we weren't stupid, and none of us wanted to die that day cause some impersonal cop was trigger-happy. Cause, I'll tell you, there have been times in our very city when an overzealous and freaked out cop shot some kid, cause he thought the kid was gonna kill him. We knew that they were necessary and all, but it seemed like they always showed up after a crime happened, instead of catching the

39

criminals in the act. And since none of us was afraid of cops, except maybe Andy, they weren't taking Jack from us without a fight.

So, there we were, a showdown in my own house with the cops who were now the enemy, and we needed a leader to take charge. The boys formed a half-circle around me, blocking the hallway. I took the lead, probably just like Jack or Brad or any of us would, puffed out my chest, and told them it was time for them to leave. That's when the yelling began.

"We're just doing our job kid, now you boys need to move out of the way."

"Bullshit! We ain't going nowhere!"

"It's none of your business kid; now get the hell out the way!"

"That's complete bullshit and you know it! Your job isn't to manipulate kids, just cause your bigger than us and cause you got guns! Your job is to protect us, and kids like Jack!"

I moved closer and so did the boys, as always, showing support for one another. That's when I started yelling at 'the boys in blue' again (which were nothing in comparison to my boys).

"Where were you guys when Jack's messed up dad beat on his mom! You obviously weren't doing your job then! Or when, after his mom was in the hospital, the prick took it out on Jack's sister and then molested her! Where were you then!

"Don't stand in my house, in front of me and my boys and call us a gang and thugs, and tell us that you're just doing your jobs! Cause that asshole deserves whatever Jack did to him! Why don't you do your precious little jobs, and protect him and his family. Oh, let me take a wild guess, you think Jack's the criminal don't you! Tell me, did you know

41

that Jack's IQ was close to 130? Damn, the kid is only our age and he's probably smarter than both of you two put together!

"Tell me another thing; do you know where Jack's mom is right now? She's in a damn mental hospital, where she goes every weekend. Or can you tell us where his little sister is now? She at the therapist cause that asshole, who you're protecting now, ruined her life! And the best you can say is that you're doing your job! That's bullshit!

"And you know what? That boy in there is as big as you are and I'll bet he's a hell of a lot tougher than you! And do you really think that after he did whatever he did to his prick of a dad that brought you here, do you think that he wouldn't do the same to you! What are you gonna do, shoot us all? Shoot us, like you did that black kid last summer! If you plan on using force on Jack, then you'd better call for back-up, or swat, cause there ain't no way you're getting past us to get to him! No way!"

"Are you done?" The younger of the two pricks said back, as I heard Mark and Paul pumping their fists into their hands and rocking back and forth on their heels. There was no way that we were gonna be intimidated by those two dipshits.

"We ain't afraid of you, but we are just as smart as you. This can get ugly or it can go smoothly, it's up to you now. If you really wanted to do your job, then you'd figure a way to make this work without any violence, but that's if you really meant that you were just doing your job.

"We can get Jack to come out and go with you, but there ain't no way you're going in there. Like I told you, the kid in there is probably the biggest one in the house and maybe the smartest. And if we tell him it's cool, then he knows it is. Cause we boys don't try to manipulate and pick on people smaller and not as smart as us, cause it's just plain wrong. So, what's it gonna be?"

Well I guess those doorknobs took their smart pills that day, cause they agreed with us and let us get Jack out. And, like they didn't believe me or something, their jaws nearly hit the floor when they saw this kid that was as big as an ox, crying and covered in his father's blood.

"Good call kid, good call," was all that the cop said as they left.

They asked if they could put cuffs on him and Jack looked at us. We told him that it was o.k. and that we'd be at the 'cop shop', before he knew it. And, we were. We called everyone that mattered, after we got there, and before it got dark Jack had one hell of a supporting cast. They kept him there for a while and then shipped him to 'Juvenile Hall', where the bad kids went.

We went to see him every day until they made us leave. Our moms all pitched in and got him a lawyer. After he had like three or four hearings, Jack got to come back home with us. Of course, we all had pretty much signed on to work our butts off for free for the next year and to get good

grades, but it was worth it. We got Jack back and he was one

of us, one of 'the boys'.

# Jeremy Aldana

## Issues
## Spring 1991

Life wasn't all that bad, even though we all had issues.

As kids, everything seemed bigger and brighter, on account

that we were smaller than grown-ups and our minds weren't

fully developed yet. However, it wasn't very hard to see

things from a grown-ups perspective, at least not for us, or so

we thought.

We were kids, and we certainly knew more than

adults ever gave us credit for. I'm sure that's why they always

say that us kids think we know it all. Well they are right for

the most part, we did know a lot. We knew about the world

and about history, and we knew about the really important

stuff about life, like friendship and values and manners and

the difference between right and wrong, even though we

couldn't articulate it like adults could.

We knew enough about adult stuff to get involved

when we wanted to, and to stay away when we knew we

should. For instance, we knew why our parents went to work every day and had the weekends off. We knew that whatever they did, they did it for money cause it cost money to have a house, and pay for food and clothes and electricity. We even knew that the water cost money. But, we also knew that it was those 'bills', as our parents called them, that were supposed to be paid by them, not us.

We knew that it was their job to provide those things for us. And, of course, we knew that raising us with love, keeping us safe, keeping the bills paid, and their own adult lives in order wasn't that easy to pull off. That's why we, for the most part, never gave them a hard time. But, we also knew that our jobs were to be kids and we weren't supposed to have to deal with those things until we got older.

In that respect, they were right, we didn't know everything. That should've been okay though, on account that we shouldn't have had to worry about adult stuff until we were ready to. But, that's how life works. You deal with the hand that you were dealt, or so that's what mom used to say.

We weren't 'ingrates' or ungrateful, cause we had a nice house in a nice neighborhood. We all knew, each one of us, that our folks were supposed to do right by us, but as we all learned way too early, that life doesn't always work out that way. So, we tried to stay kids as long as we could and enjoy every moment that we could.

We wanted to be like the other kids our age, immature and silly, with no cares in the world. We didn't want to be left out, so we latched onto each other and never let go. We tried being kids while we were forced to be young adults and that's when problems happened, cause no one taught us how to be adults.

It was like an art form, for the boys and me, to learn how to be young adults. We had to learn from watching our parents, and be able to take out the good parts from a heap of bad ones. I guess that's why we understood each other so well, cause we were all that we had, we thought.

Brad missed his sister a lot, and it changed him and his parents. Paul's parents forgot his last birthday. Jack's dad was in prison and always called collect, even though not one call was ever accepted. His sister was in therapy and his mom still went to the nuthouse every weekend for treatment and medication. Mark thought he'd never be tall enough or big enough to fit in anywhere. He fought every kid that looked at him the wrong way, and even got himself kicked out of Junior High. Despite all of our own issues, I still think Andy had it worst of all.

As far as feelings were concerned, Andy had it worse than all of us, cause even though each of us had our own issues, we seemed to be loved more or less. He was the brainiac of the group, the most logical one, and the one who longed for approval the most. He was a scrawny kid and that didn't help his case out much. But, any one of us would've told you that there wasn't a nicer kid around.

Andy's parents seemed to hate him and told him as much every chance they had. They didn't come out and say "I hate you" but it was implied when they never said "I love you," to him. They had plenty of opportunities to tell him they cared about him, but they never did.

Andy was the one who we all thought would spend the least amount of time at home, but it was the exact opposite. He was the one who was at home the most, despite feeling not wanted there. None of us would wish that on our worst enemy, which was by far Jack's prick of a dad, who we were all glad to see locked up behind bars.

I think that Andy was probably the toughest kid I'd ever known, maybe even tougher (in a different way) than Jack, cause none of us ever understood how he managed to smile every day. It was clear to all of us, that Andy's mom and dad never liked him that much. Either he was doing everything wrong in their eyes or he was merely an annoyance

to them. That sort of thing does a number on a kid.

Can you say, "Complex?" Andy's constant longing for

approval was sad, cause we knew he was better than that. It,

by far, outweighed Mark's constant longing to be accepted.

Andy's mom used to pick him up from school when

we were younger and the only thing that changed about that,

was that one day she just stopped showing up. She never told

him sorry, not one time. Andy sometimes waited until well

after dinner before he'd call one of us to go get him. Usually,

one of us would have our folks drive to the school to pick

him up.

I once asked mom, why Andy's mom would always

tell him that she'd be there even though she never was. Mom

told me that everybody was different, and that everybody's

priorities were different as well. And, even though your kids

were supposed to come first in your lives, some people just

never got that. We got it alright, though. That's why we were always there for him, and would always be. He was safe with us and didn't have to worry about approval anymore, but I'm not totally sure he ever really understood that.

Whenever he thought of something brilliant or scored well on his tests, it was us that he told. He even showed us his report cards, and then he put them away in a shoebox under his bed. The shoebox was where he kept all of his important awards and papers, which his parents never cared to see. Kids weren't supposed to have to deal with that, they were supposed to be loved and cherished. I think someone forgot to tell his mom and dad that along the way.

Andy seemed to be a burden to his parents, what with all the food his skinny little body took in and the ripped up clothes that were full of holes. He taught himself how to wash his own clothes, which actually worked out for us, cause he then taught us. He had to check his own homework and even had to borrow money from Brad to buy an alarm clock, cause his parents were always gone before he'd wake up. He also taught himself how to cook and made his own lunches.

Jack had an idea one day, in the spring before my family's accident. He said we should camp out one night and follow Andy's parents to find out why they always left before he woke up. We all wanted to know just as bad as Jack did, but we understood why Jack was so angry. Jack didn't have parents anymore as far as he was concerned and hated the fact that Andy had both parents, but neither of them amounted to very much. We all approved, and like Jack's idea. We all swore never to tell Andy what we were doing, but Jack was right, something had to be done and we knew his idea had a shot at success.

# Jeremy Aldana

## The Stakeout (Part I)
## Flashback to Spring 1990

We all camped out in my backyard on Sunday night

and each of us brought an extra pair of clothes. We'd decided

that we'd follow Andy's parents, and then we'd go get him,

and take him to school. We knew he'd love to have us do

that; and so it began.

None of us talked about what we were going to do in

the next few hours. But, if you were to look at any of us

sitting in the circle, in the middle of the tent that night, you

would've known that we were all thinking about it. And of

course, we knew it wouldn't be too long before Paul would

break the silence with some kind of joke.

"Hey, maybe his parent's are secret agents and they

aren't really his parents at all. You know like they were on

assignment and they weren't allowed to interact with him. Or

maybe, just maybe, Andy was part of some government secret

experiment to find out what would happen to a kid who

received no love or interaction from his parents. Yea, maybe Andy was secretly being molded into a super-warrior who is made to have no feelings and then sent off to war in some foreign country or some distant planet!"

"Yea right, Paul! Maybe they're waiting to see what it takes and how long it takes to make a kid snap, and become a serial killer!"

"Knock it off, Jack!"

"Oh, what do you know, Mark? At least you have parents, Andy's are a joke, and we all know he'd be better off without them!"

I think Brad was getting mad, cause he hollered at all of us, and he didn't usually yell.

"All of you shut up, this is stupid! We all know Andy is messed up, just like the rest of us. That's why we're the boys, cause all of us have messed up folks. But sitting here making up crap about Andy's parents is useless and we don't need to fight about it. In a couple of hours, we'll find out why they are so messed up, and then we can fight about what to

do. We should be getting mad at them, and not each other.

And you Jack, should understand that better than any of us.

"Heck, I ain't seen my pops for over two weeks and

when I do see my mom, she's either high or coming down off

of one. Paul, your parents barely remember your name! And

when was the last time they hugged you, or tucked you in to

bed? Mark, your folks talk to you like your some punk kid

keying their cars and stealing hubcaps. And, Jack, your dad's

in prison and your sister isn't even coherent anymore. As for

your mom, when she is home, she's all drugged up on lithium

and walks around like a zombie all the time.

"We boys all got problems, and that's why we've got

to stick together. When we're older and away from this

craziness, we will owe our lives and our sanity to each other.

If we didn't have each other, then we'd all feel like Andy does

and I know we deserve better, even if we're the only ones to

know it."

# BOYS WILL BE BOYS

Mom always said that family came first and that the most important part of life was telling the people you love, that you love them. She said that we had to let them know that they are loved. All we had to do was look at Andy, to prove that mom was right.

None of us slept that night. After Brad's speech, we all sat in silence for a while and really thought hard about what he'd said. He was right, you know, we weren't the enemy. It was those who treated us like we didn't exist, they were the enemy. We never wanted to hurt anyone unless they hurt us first.

After about an hour, I decided to break the silence and turned on my flashlight.

"Hey guys, remember when Paul was making Shannon laugh all lunch hour, and then that jerk Matt went after him?"

Everybody started laughing and then each told their side of the story as they remembered it.

Paul started first. "Yea, I was on a roll. The head cheerleader, who just happened to be the prettiest girl in the whole school, was actually talking to me!"

"At least she wasn't puking!" Jack threw out one of his patented burns.

"Whatever," Paul kept going, "there I was, telling her the one about the Easter Bunny, Santa Claus, and the Smart Blonde. You know, how they all have one thing in common!"

"Let me guess, genius, none of them exist. That is such a stupid joke, you're lucky she has brown hair," I said, laughing the whole time.

"She was eating out of my hands and I was on a roll. After that went over as a hit, you know I made the mistake of asking her if she knew that Matt dyed his hair brown and that he was actually a blonde. And of course, Matt happened to be standing behind me. Can you say 'Up the Creek'! It sure was a good thing that you guys were there."

"You bet your butt, it was a good thing," Brad added.

# BOYS WILL BE BOYS

Mark then went on from there, "Yea, and then he looked down at you, and I knew you were in trouble, big-time! And then we all looked at each other, and were like 'Oh, Shit'!"

"Yea, it just got funnier after that," Jack started in again. "First of all, I had no idea your skinny little butt could move that fast. I mean, when you got up, I was like wow, was that Paul? Did any of you guys know he could move that fast?"

A solid round of 'no's' filled the tent.

"Yea," I took over where Jack left off. "And then when that jerk Matt slipped on Mr. Cumming's wet floor, hit the ground, and slid into your feet Jack, I thought for sure he was gonna cry! Does Shannon still talk to you after that, she was Matt's girl you know?"

"Yea, she smiles at me in the hall and says hello sometimes."

# Jeremy Aldana

"So, is anybody tired?" I asked. I wanted to break the new silence that followed Paul's story. Unfortunately, I didn't have to, cause it wasn't a second after that, when we heard the tent unzip. We stared, wide-eyed at the zipper, and watched Andy get in the tent, none of us making a sound.

"What's up guys? Why didn't anybody tell me that we were camping out? What, am I not allowed, ain't I one of the boys? And what one of the boys does, all of the boys do. Right?"

"Yea, of course, Andy, get in here. You got your flashlight?" Brad asked, as he moved closer to me to make room for Andy.

"What's going on guys, why is everyone so quiet?"

And of course, every single one of the boys looked right at me, like suddenly I was the group's spokesman. I knew adults had awkward silences and I remember even Jacob had them, when he was around cute girls, but this was my first one. Apparently, I had the boys to thank for that.

# BOYS WILL BE BOYS

What was I going to say to him? 'Hey Andy, we think your parents suck and we think that they're horrible people. So, we were gonna spy on them, but hey, it's all for you'. I was nowhere near the end of my thought, when Andy brought me back.

"Well, what is it?"

"Thanks guys," I said in a sarcastic voice, as I stared at them for a half second each.

"Andy, where are your parents?"

"They're at home, why?"

"Where do they go in the morning, before you get up?"

Just like I figured, the boys were gonna let me field this one, all on my own.

"They go to work."

"And where are they, when you get home from school?"

"At work still, you know double shifts and all that stuff."

We all knew that was a bunch of crap, but the boys wouldn't dare be that truthful right now, even though Brad had no problem being deadly honest earlier. But Brad would've said that he only did that, cause we were fighting, and of course we would've agreed with him, cause it was tough to stay mad at Brad.

I couldn't look directly at Andy, not right then, anyway.

"Andy, do you know what they do for a living?"

"No, do any of you guys know what your folks do for a living?"

It was as if someone flipped a switch on the boys, cause a second after Andy asked the question, answers started pouring in, one by one. I heard Jack first.

"My dad's a convict, and my mom's on disability from the state."

Mark went next, "My dad works at the brewery, and my mom is a waitress."

Paul went next, "My dad works at the brewery too, and my mom is a stay-at-home mom."

Brad followed Paul, as the boys went in turn, like how they sat in the circle. Brad picked up his head like he was proud or something, like he was in 'AA' for kids.

"My dad's a truck driver, and my mom is a drug addict."

And then it was my turn, but Andy saved me the grief.

"O.k., so I don't know what my parents do, is that a crime?"

And again, the boys looked at me.

"O.k. Andy, you're one of the boys right?"

"Yea, of course I am."

"And we boys don't lie to each other, right?"

"Right."

"Well, we didn't expect you to be here tonight, cause we were gonna get up early, or as it stands now stay up late, and find out where your folks go in the mornings."

We didn't have a contingency plan or anything, cause we didn't think Andy would show up like this, but I can guarantee you that what Andy said next, none of us were ready for.

"I'm in, how can I help?"

It was in that moment that it felt like someone had lifted a car off our shoulders, and we all looked at each other and smiled.

Brad stated first, on account that he looked most ready.

"Okay Andy, do your folks ever leave one of their cars at home and do you know about what time they leave the house?"

"They must take both cars, cause when I leave they're both gone. And as far as when they leave, I'm not sure, I just try not to think about it. I just accept it, cause at least I have a bed to sleep in."

The second Andy answered Brad; we were ready for Jack to go off. And, as always, he was right on cue.

"You just accept it! That's crap Andy, and you know it!"

"Yea, Jack, I know it. And I appreciate that you care, but I get it. Come on Jack! You know me. Yea, I'm scrawny and sort of geeky and all, but what, you don't think I'm mad at them. But what can I do about it, Jack?"

Brad waited for the silence to take over again and started once more.

"By the way Andy, what do you mean sort of? You are full-blown geek, but we still got your back."

"Yea, way back, right?"

"Seriously though Andy, is there anything you can tell us that will help?"

Andy went on to tell us about the time when he woke up one morning after hearing sounds coming from downstairs. He told us that he got his Louisville Slugger, which he only got on account that Jack got one and he looked up to Jack for his toughness. He said that he headed downstairs 'tiptoeing' the whole way.

He said he heard his dad telling his mom to hurry up, cause they wanted to get out of the house before he woke up. He said it was surreal, whatever that meant, like he was in some movie or something. He told us that he felt like he was dreaming his worst fears. We told him to turn his flashlight off, cause we could see he was fighting back tears and none of us felt that he should have to do this with all of us staring at him.

Even though we were the boys, we were still boys waiting to become men. And, just like the women of the fifty's, boys weren't supposed to cry in front of others, especially other boys. Everyone knew that boys cry, but for some weird reason we weren't allowed to or else we were

seen as weak. It didn't make sense to us why adults held their

tears inside and then made us boys do the same, in order to

be accepted.

We knew that everyone got sad and mad, and isn't

crying the way that we let out those feelings. Aren't we

supposed to let them out around others, so they can make us

feel better? Isn't that what friends and family were for?

We knew we had to survive in this world, after all, we

were only kids, and we all had the rest of our lives in front of

us. But because we were the boys and we all knew this, we

just tried to make it easier on each other. So, when we all

made the gesture to turn off our flashlights and not dwell on

the fact that Andy was dying inside, we let him know that we

were there with him and that we understood. Again, kids

don't know shit, right? Well, we at least knew how to care for

each other.

# Jeremy Aldana

It started to get light out as Andy finished telling us about his walking nightmare. He said he stood at the top of the stairs, watched them leave the house, and then saw his dad run back into the house to get his keys. He said his dad just looked at him and then left. He said he then ran down the stairs and watched them both leave. He said he went back to bed and never spoke of it again, until now. Now, he just sleeps until the last minute cause that way he doesn't have to see them hurt him. He said it was easier that way.

Brad cleared his throat and took a deep breath to talk, cause he'd been crying too. There was no doubt that we all had been crying, cause after Brad cleared his throat we all did too, and a round of sniffles soon filled the tent.

"It's alright you guys," Andy said as he laughed and sniffled too.

"Do you remember what time that was?" Brad continued, after he recovered.

"Yea, I think it was either five o'clock or six o'clock."

# BOYS WILL BE BOYS

"Guys we gotta get ready to go now, cause it's 4:30."

One by one, we all filed out of the tent and into the house to change, none of us saying a word to each other.

We were like warriors preparing to go into battle. We were scared to find out the truth, on account that we knew we shouldn't have to do this, cause his parents should've cared more. But we were focused, and with the sobbing out of the way, we thought we were ready.

# Jeremy Aldana

## The Stakeout (Part II)
### 'Contingency Plan'
### Flashback to Spring 1990

Andy didn't live too far from me, only a few blocks
away, and we weren't stupid; we knew that we weren't old
enough to drive yet, and that if we took our bikes we
would've probably been seen. That's why we woke up Jake,
even though he didn't much like the idea. He agreed though,
cause he knew Andy and didn't like how his parents treated
him almost as much as we didn't like it.

He was my brother, and brothers were supposed to
be there for each other. Besides, he just got his license and
driving was an opportunity that he didn't pass up too much.
We had to promise that we'd do his chores for two weeks,
which was fine by us.

Jake said that he had to take a quick shower and that
he'd meet us at the end of Andy's block, in a few minutes.
After we saw Andy's parents split up, we knew we'd never be
able to follow them both, so we changed plans.

70

# BOYS WILL BE BOYS

When Jake met us at the end of the block, we told him that we weren't going to be able to follow them both and that we'd all have to go with him. Jake said that he'd never trailed someone before, but had seen enough movies to know how not to be seen. He said that since Andy's parents didn't know his car and that they wouldn't be expecting us to follow them, it shouldn't be too difficult. He said that he just hoped we knew what we were doing. We thought we did, anyway.

Jack and Mark sat in the backseat, with Andy between them. Brad, Jake, and me were up front. Paul volunteered to ride in the very back, in the hatch, even though Mark should've sat back there cause he's the smallest one. Paul wanted to be nice and didn't want to make Mark go through that. We told Andy to sit in the middle, cause if his parents saw any of us in the car it would be hard for them to see who was in the middle of the backseat.

It was Brad's idea to follow Andy's mom first, and we agreed, cause Brad seemed to be the most logical one at the moment. We thought that Andy was in no shape to make those kinds of decisions. Sure he was eager and said that he was fine, but we knew better. We all knew him well enough to know that when he was nervous or scared, he always acted tougher than he was. None of us blamed him though, after all, he wasn't even supposed to be here. He was fighting back, even if it was in his own way, and we were all proud of him for it.

Us kids, react to things more than we do anything else, on account that we have so little control of our own lives. And, reacting is exhausting in every way. The crazy part was that we worried about how others would react, only so we wouldn't have to react later. And, Andy was reacting to us caring, to us doing something for him. When a kid constantly reacts, adjusts, and adapts, he doesn't have time to worry about what will happen the next day.

Kids react differently to things than adults do, cause kids see the world as a great big place full of unlimited opportunities and adventures. Adults, as far as we knew, saw the world as one big routine after another. But the reason kids are so dramatic about everything, is cause when they react to everything, day in and day out, they grow accustom to those reactions and take each moment head on with all their energy and focus.

Adults spend all their time completing their routines, and for whatever reasons they choose to give all of their energy to one thing, some to another, and even less to others. Adults call them priorities and kids always view those priorities as being messed up, cause they are never at the top of them. And, that's why we were here, following Andy's mom, cause we knew her priorities were messed up and we wanted to know why.

We figured it would be easy enough not to draw too much attention to us, even at five in the morning, on account of Jake's car. He had a 1984 Subaru that he bought from a friend the summer before. It wasn't that big, but we knew it would do the trick. Me and Brad had it worse, I think, cause we had to squeeze into a seat that was made for only one person, not two. It wasn't too bad though, cause we weren't that big, we barely weighed a hundred twenty five pounds each.

Brad sat on the inside, away from the door and I had the window, while the boys fit comfortably in the back. As we drove behind Andy's mom, what Jake had said earlier echoed in my head: "I hope you know what you're doing." I honestly think he was right in doubting our plan, cause I don't think we knew exactly what we were doing. We just knew that Andy was suffering, and we were his boys.

It only took a few blocks of driving when Mark tapped me on the shoulder and pointed back, for me to look. Mark was telling me to look, cause Andy was passed out cold, sleeping on Jack's shoulder and Jack hadn't socked him yet. Jack certainly wasn't the 'touchy-feely' kind, but he definitely had a soft spot where Andy was concerned.

# BOYS WILL BE BOYS

Jake did a good job of following Andy's mom, and so far, she had only stopped once to get some coffee. When I looked at the clock in the car it only read 5:20 and I asked Jake if it was right, cause it seemed like we had been in the car for hours. His response was classic Jake, "I picked you up at five didn't I?"

I let it go without a comeback, on account that we needed him and we were glad he was there for us.

After she got her coffee, she drove downtown and parked in a parking structure that belonged to a hotel, one of the largest in the city. Me and Brad looked at each other with complete confusion in our eyes, as Jake parked across the street, got out, and put a quarter in the meter. He suggested that we all get out and get some coffee.

We weren't used to drinking coffee, but we knew he needed it and maybe Andy too. Besides, this might be a good time to start for all of us, cause even though me, Brad, and

Paul were wide awake, Mark, Andy, and Jack seemed to be pretty much asleep.

Luckily, for us, there was a Dunkin' Donuts across the street from the hotel, and Jake said that they had food as well as coffee. He said he'd buy us breakfast and we wouldn't have to pay him back. That's when I gave him a hug. It was while I was hugging him, that he told me that once we got inside, me and him needed to sit alone, cause he needed to tell me something.

Jake told the boys to get some breakfast and for Andy to get some coffee. He told them that since this was about Andy's mom, then Andy should be awake for this. The boys agreed, ordered croissant rolls and OJ, and joked around like this was any other day. Jake and me watched from the booth behind them, on account that they sat at the counter. As we ate our food, Jake asked me to tell him everything about Andy and about our plan. I told him everything, and that's

when he asked me if I had ever heard about that hotel Andy's
mom went into.

"The Charleston?"

"Yea, do you know anything about it?"

"Not really, I mean I know that it's like one of the
biggest hotels in the city, but I take it that you're going to tell
me more."

"Well, little bro, I just hope she's a clerk or
something, and not a cleaning lady."

I didn't want to ask too many questions about what
Jake was talking about, so I did my best just to listen.

"O.k. Jake, I'm listening."

"Well, little bro, I'm not 100% positive or anything,
but word at school and at the parties is that the cleaning
ladies at The Charleston, are escorts. They really aren't
cleaning ladies bro; that's just their cover."

Okay, Jake had me confused now, on account that I
had no idea what an escort was, or what they had to do with

cleaning ladies. I knew that cleaning ladies at hotels went into the guest rooms when the guests checked out and cleaned them, but that was all I knew. I probably didn't have to ask him anything, cause I'm sure he could read my face, but I couldn't help myself.

"O.k. what the hell is an escort?"

"Come on little bro, you don't know?"

"No, I don't, am I suppose to?"

"Okay, little man, time for a very important lesson. Go up to the counter, get a phone book and ask to use their phone. On your way back, have Jack come back to the booth with us so he can keep an eye on the hotel in case Andy's mom leaves."

After bringing back Jack, the phone book, and the restaurants' cordless phone, I watched Jake flip through the yellow pages to the letter 'E'. It took another two page turns to find the word escorts. He told me to pick anyone of them and call them. I asked him what was I suppose to say, and he told me to first deepen my voice and act like I knew what I was talking about.

What Jake told me next, was as much of a shock to me as it was to Jack, who stopped looking out the window. He told me to ask them how much it would cost for a date with the woman of my choice, and if that price included sex. Good ole' brother Jake was nice enough to reach across the table and push my chin back up to its normal upright position. So, I did as he said, dialed 'AAA Escorts', and cleared my throat.

# Jeremy Aldana

## The Stakeout (Part III)
## 'AAA Escorts'
## Flashback to Spring 1990

"AAA Escorts, the safest and most discreet dates in town. My name is Barbara, how can I help you, today?"

Before the woman with the sweetest voice I ever heard finished her greeting, I felt my heart start to pound and barely heard Jake telling me to calm down and maintain. It was go time and show time, and I knew I had to play the role of my life. I cleared my throat one more time, and mentally pretended to be an older guy looking for a discreet date inside a phone book.

"Ah yes, Barbara, I've never done this before, so please bear with me."

"Of course, sir, how can I help you today?"

"Well, like I said, I'm new to this and all."

"New to what, sir?"

I cleared my throat yet again and pushed Jack away from me, on account that he was inches from my face. He was desperately trying to listen to Barbara, like he'd never heard a grown up woman talk before.

"Well, new to paying for a date, well I mean paying for a date with a woman I don't know."

"Well, sir, I can certainly understand. I am going to do everything possible to make this experience a comfortable one for you."

"Thank you, Barbara."

"Okay sir, are you local?"

"No. Well, yes. I mean, I'm not from around here but I am here in town right now. If that's what you mean."

"Yes, sir, that's what I was looking for. Where are you lodging, while on your stay?"

"I'm staying at The Charleston, downtown"

"Okay, that's great; we have a few ladies that work down there quite a bit."

As Barbara asked me about what kind of woman I was interested in spending the day or evening with, I looked up to find that the boys had all made their way back to me. No doubt, Jack told them what was going on, even though I had no clue. I told Barbara that I was only looking to figure out costs and options, and that I planned to call her back in a while.

I asked if she had a woman who had blonde hair, blue eyes, was in her thirty's, classy, attractive, and looked like a woman who might have a family (an almost perfect description of Andy's mom). I also asked her about where me and my date would meet, and how much everything would cost.

She told me that the woman would meet me at my hotel room, and that I would be charged in two-hour blocks. She also told me that she had a lovely woman who matched my interests, almost perfectly. After that, I asked her about what me and my date were allowed to do. And even though I knew that I wouldn't call back, I still felt a little weird about asking her. Despite my uneasiness, I listened as she told me that the date would be very discreet, and that I would have to discuss those details with her when she got to my room.

She went on to tell me that some clients just wanted to talk and some wanted more, but that the dates were the same, so I didn't need to worry about anything.

"Again, sir, it's very discreet."

Barbara finished and said that she'd be looking forward to my call later, to confirm. I thanked her and hung up, only to hear the boys ask me about a million questions at once.

Jake told the boys to calm down, and it didn't surprise me that they listened. They all scrunched in the small booth next to me. Jake then said it again, "Hope she's a clerk at that hotel, and not a cleaning lady."

I told him thanks for the lesson and he just smiled.

"See, little bro, there's more about this world you live in, than you know."

Jeremy Aldana

Me and the boys, we knew about sex alright, but never was it like this. Never had any of us talked to an older woman about sex. We had crushes, and the occasional two-week girlfriend that never really meant anything. The most we knew was only first and second base. None of us even knew what third base consisted of, but we sure had our ideas.

Jake said that we needed to find out what Andy's mom was doing there. And, no sooner had Jake finished getting our attention, did Jack shout above the group.

"She's leaving guys, she's leaving!"

We had to decide quickly what we were going to do. Were we going to follow her, or go to the hotel and find out why she was there? So, we all did the same thing, at the same time; we all looked to my brother Jake.

## The Stakeout (Part IV)
## 'Close Call'
## Flashback to Spring 1990

Jake did as I hoped he would, and took command. He said that she'd been at the hotel for about an hour, and it didn't look good. He said that we could check back with the hotel later, but that we should follow her now and see where she goes next.

Me and the boys all ran out to the car and Jake paid the bill. We all piled in the same way we got out before. There wasn't any time for calling 'shotgun', which of course worked in favor of me and Brad, especially since the boys were all now wide awake. Jake had taught me how to start the car, and how to turn on the blinkers. He also taught me about the gas and brake pedals. I think he used me as a study partner, on account that he had to take his driving test three times before he passed it.

Jack, our resident scout, was nearly foaming at the mouth, hitting the glass and telling us that she was driving

85

away. Brad spoke up first, in response to Jack. "Calm down Jack, or you might piss yourself." Everyone got a good laugh and Brad got 'the finger' from Jack.

We took off quickly, once Jake got in the car and were only a block behind Andy's mom. We were all amazed to find out that Andy's mom had only driven about a mile from The Charleston, when we watched her pull into the parking lot of another hotel.

'The Palace Inn,' the sign read, as we pulled alongside the curb across the street from where Andy's mom parked her car. Again, Jake got out, put a quarter in the meter, and told us that we should get out and look for a place to sit.

This hotel was nothing in comparison to The Charleston. It would be like comparing Ritz Crackers to generic supermarket brand saltines. The Charleston had several floors and was a large establishment, whereas The Palace Inn looked rundown and neglected. It had an office that was separate from the rooms, which sat above the

parking lot, in a horseshoe like design.

Andy's mom was dressed in a cleaning maid's

uniform, the same one that she was wearing when she left

The Charleston, when she walked into the check-in lobby.

Now that we knew that Andy's mom was in fact a cleaning

lady, it confirmed that there was an even greater chance that

she might be an escort. We still hoped that she was just a

cleaning lady, for Andy's sake, but I think that Andy hoped

that more than any of us.

Luckily, for us, we found a coffee shop just a few

buildings away from our car. Jake bought us all coffee and we

watched as Andy's mom went into one room after another,

only spending about ten to fifteen minutes in each. Jake

pointed out that at every room she went into, someone

opened the door and let her in. Jake told us that normally,

when a cleaning lady cleans a room, the guests have already

checked out and wouldn't be able to let her in.

Jake was ordering his second coffee, when Jack spoke up again. "Guys, she coming this way. Guys, she's coming this way. Right now!"

Jake was at least fifteen feet away, at the counter, and wouldn't be able to do much for us at this point.

"Jack, how much time we got?"

"About thirty seconds, maybe a minute at the most!"

I knew we couldn't go out the front and I didn't see any backdoor, but I knew we had to do something quick. "Alright guys, everybody in the bathroom. Now!"

I hoped the bathroom was big enough for all of us, and empty. The bathroom was at the end of the counter, to the right of where Jake was waiting for his coffee. I looked up to see Jake with a puzzled look on his face. I quickly turned around, almost running into the counter when I heard him calling my name.

"What!"

"What are you guys doing?"

"That's her, Jake!" I pointed, behind him, to the front door and saw Andy's mom reaching for the handle.

"Get us when she's gone, bro."

"Alright, little man, alright."

I didn't have to tell the boys to keep quiet this time, which was surprising to say the least. I guess they knew how important it was that Andy's mom not see us. Me and Brad stood at the door and pushed it open a crack, just enough to see Jake and Andy's mom at the counter. But not so much that they'd see us. And, since Jake knew we were in here, I knew he wouldn't do anything to blow our cover.

Me and Brad watched and listened as best as we could, to Jake and Andy's mom talking. I wondered what they were saying, cause we couldn't hear them too well. We really only heard noises that sounded like voices talking. A lot of thoughts passed through my mind in those few minutes, standing on the inside of the bathroom door with all the boys watching me.

Maybe Andy's mom was actually an escort, which might be reason enough for her to not tell Andy. Or maybe she actually was a hotel cleaning lady, which might be another reason not to tell Andy. I knew we'd eventually figure it all out, one way or another, but I couldn't think of any reason why Jake starting talking to her.

Andy's mom was what we all called 'a looker'. She was a pretty lady who seemed decent enough, that is unless you were her kid. Andy could easily attest to that. And I knew my brother well enough to know that when a pretty woman was around, he usually went into 'the zone'.

We used to joke with him and amongst ourselves, that when Jake went into 'the zone' it was all over. The girls never stood a chance. Jake had the good looks and the charm, complete with a mustache and goatee. He was five feet ten inches tall, weighed about two hundred pounds, and charming words just flowed past his pearly white teeth. What concerned me about this situation, in particular, was that

Andy's mom was an attractive older woman and just his type.

I could hardly wait to be just like him.

Me and Brad pushed the door open, when we no

longer heard them talking. We then looked at each other in

disbelief, as we watched Jake and Andy's mom walk out the

front door together. We pushed the door wide open for the

boys, as we watched Jake set his keys down on our table. I

don't know why he left his keys for us, cause none of us

could drive, let alone drive a stick-shift.

Jake and Andy's mom got into her car and drove

away. We all decided to walk back to my house, even though

it was quite a distance from where we were. We figured since

school was out of the question, and there was no way we'd be

able to follow them, we didn't have much else to do. That's

what me and Brad thought, anyway.

It was Jack, Mark, and Andy that decided we should

walk over to The Palace Inn, and find out what Andy's mom

was doing there. Then walk the mile or so back to The

Charleston and do the same. And wouldn't you know it, Andy seemed to snap back into rare form by telling us that we should make sure that we come back every hour and fill the meter, so Jake's car wouldn't get towed.

Andy said that Jake would come back for his car later. He said, and I guess he was right, that no self-respecting owner of a car and a license would take such freedoms for granted. And that maybe we shouldn't go home after all, but instead leave a note in the car that told Jake to wait for us, cause we'd be checking back every hour.

# BOYS WILL BE BOYS

## The Stakeout (Part V)
### 'Greenfield Avenue'
### Flashback to Spring 1990

Me and the boys were unsuccessful in obtaining any information from the clerk at The Palace Inn, and headed back to the car when we saw Jake. He was coming out of the coffee shop with yet another coffee. We all looked around to make sure that Andy's mom wasn't with him, and then ran across the street. The boys all ran to him and started asking him questions, while me and Andy went to the car instead. I could only imagine what Andy must've been thinking. I think that I was the only one to notice that Jake had been gone for exactly one hour.

Me, Andy, Jake, and the boys all piled back into Jake's car and drove away. Jack was the first to speak after we were on the road.

"What did you find out, Jake, where to next?"

"I'll tell you guys when we get there."

After Jake's answer, we all sat in silence until we arrived at the corner of 92$^{nd}$ and Greenfield Avenue. We all knew the block well, though we hadn't been there for at least a year.

During the summers, we'd walk everywhere we could around town. We'd walk down to County Stadium, then up to State Fair Park, then back up to 92$^{nd}$, and then over to Lincoln Avenue. We knew the city like the back of our hands, but Greenfield Avenue was the best of them all. There was the movie theater where we used to sneak in to watch two shows. We'd go in and pay for the first show and then after it was over, we'd sneak into the second one.

There was the 'Ma and Pop' store where we used to buy penny candies and bottles of soda. Jack got caught one summer, stealing a penny candy and was told to never come back.

There was a magic shop on the block where we used to buy joke props and stuff. Things like hand buzzers and fake ice cubes with flies in them. There was a bowling alley slash bar, which none of us ever went inside. There was also a butcher shop, midway down the block, and a beauty salon across the street from it.

There was a series of buildings that were right next to each other, side by side, that kinda looked like one big building. They were called 'Strip Malls'. The strip mall was the one place we all went, whenever we had money. And, it never failed, that we would always leave with no money. It had a take-out pizza place, a haircut place, and our favorite store in the world, the card shop.

The card shop was the place where grown men got to act like children, and get paid for it. But they weren't always cool though, on account that sometimes they would take advantage of some kids. They would sometimes even take advantage of unsuspecting mothers who would stop in to buy their sons some cards. And, of course, the one who got ripped off didn't even know it. They were the ones that Jack laughed at the most.

It was kind of an unwritten rule that mother's just didn't go into card shops. We used to hang out for hours at a time there. They had a table in there where it was convenient for a kid to buy a pack of cards, open it, get a good one, and then take it back up to the counter and trade it in for a another pack or a single card out of the case.

Believe it or not, there was a certain way to open a pack of cards. The wrong way was like handing your money over to someone and getting nothing in return. The right way was the careful way. You had to lay the pack on the table, face down, and open it like you would open a bag of chips. Then, you only opened it that way a little bit, until there was an opening. After that, you carefully opened the pack from the opening you made. You opened it like you would open a slice of cheese from its wrapper, careful not to rip the slice. Except with cards, you were careful not to bend the corners.

# BOYS WILL BE BOYS

It was the case though, that we all were in awe of. It was like being inches from a pirate's buried treasure. Inside the case, each card had its own protective sleeve, and some even were protected by their own glass. Like the Michael Jordan rookie card with the Bulls. They were incased in their own mini vault of glass, complete with reinforcing screws. They were the ones that were worth more money than we'd ever seen.

The case had cards that ranged from ten dollars to thousands of dollars. For instance, there was usually a Bo Jackson baseball card, the 1986 Topps one, in his KC jersey, in its own glass. Or, there was usually an Upper Deck Series 1 1989 Griffey Jr. rookie card also with its own case. But, like I mentioned, the Jordan rookie was the most prized possession for us by far.

All the greats were there in the case, from Joe Montana's rookie card to the Magic Johnson, Dr. J, and Larry

Bird card from the Topps 1980-1981 set, where all three were on the same card.

We used to hear stories about Hammerin' Hank Aaron, Mr. October Reggie Jackson, Joltin' Joe DiMaggio, and the Sultan of Swat (Babe Ruth) having cards that sold for thousands and hundreds of thousands of dollars. We'd hear that people would buy houses with them. Like one day, someone would be cleaning out their attic, and find their dad's card collection. The next thing you know their rich. I didn't know what a house cost, but I knew it was probably a lot.

As far as autographs went, they were definitely the cream of the crop. The ones on the bottom shelf of the case, the ones that were so valuable they had no price tag on them. We'd sit and listen to the dealers complaining about the ballplayers that would purposely bend a corner of the card they signed for some kid, so the dealer couldn't sell it for big money. Though we had respect for those ball players who did that, the dealers would always find some poor sap to buy it, bent corners and all.

They had it all wrong, the dealers; they would always try to make money from the game, while us kids just wanted to be important to those players. Sometimes we'd go to the ballpark up to three hours before the game to watch BP (Batting Practice), and hope to meet our favorite player.

We'd hope that maybe we could shake his hand, tell him that he was our favorite, and maybe get him to sign a ball. We made it a rule to never ask for an autograph on a card, on account that we didn't want the ball players, our heroes, thinking that we were getting them for a dealer.

Meeting our favorite baseball player was about the most awesome thing me and the boys got to do. It wasn't like meeting a celebrity or movie star, but it was like meeting a long lost brother who found a way to make it big in the world. It was really about the attention, cause it wasn't like we went around town saying "I met Rockin' Robin Yount!" It was cool meeting your favorite ball player and the dugout was like 'Never-Never Land'.

We could only dream to step inside the dugout or the bullpen for that matter. If we paid four dollars, we could get a bleacher seat, catch homerun balls, and talk to the pitchers during the game. Most of them were pretty cool, on account that they talked to us even though they didn't have to.

These guys, these baseball players, were our heroes. Not like the heroes on cartoons, but from real life, cause they were living our dreams for us. They were showing us that if they could do it, then so could we. They were approachable and they understood that the game they were playing was just as much fun for them as it was for us.

I couldn't tell you how much fun we had every summer spending the day at the ballpark, unless you were to go with us. If you were to ask any of us, at any time, what the best part of our childhood was, we would all tell you the same thing; a day at the ballpark, watching our Brewers.

# BOYS WILL BE BOYS

Football was a close second and basketball an even closer third, but nothing came close to baseball. In our neighborhood, none of us kids wanted to be a doctor or a Fireman, or a policeman; we all wanted to be professional ball players. None of us boys ever went to games with our dads, like other kids we saw there, but even that couldn't phase us on game days.

# Jeremy Aldana

## The Stakeout (Part VI)
## 'Go Joe!'
## Flashback to Spring 1990

I wondered what the boys were thinking when Jake turned off the car, and we sat there on the corner of our childhood. Greenfield Avenue housed many of our best memories, and a few of our worst ones. We'd spent a lot of our childhood on Greenfield Avenue, one way or another, and for that reason it's a place we'll never forget.

Jake broke the silence and told us why we were here. He also commented on how we used to hang out here, like he was reading my mind or something. He wasn't exactly a grown-up yet, but he had plenty more responsibilities than most kids his age had. He was what you would call 'grown-up for his age', or 'very mature'. He usually acted like an adult, as far as we were concerned, most of the time anyway, on account that he did have his moments when he let himself be a kid again. He also had his 'big-brother/best bud' moments, and none of us blamed him for anything.

# BOYS WILL BE BOYS

Jake told us that Andy's dad worked at the butcher's shop, down the block on Greenfield Avenue. He said that Andy's dad was ashamed that he wasn't a better provider for Andy and his mom, and that's why he never told Andy about his job. Jake said that Andy's mom was a housekeeper, but her jobs change all the time, on account that she worked for a 'temp agency' (whatever that was). He told us that she was also embarrassed about her job, and that was why she never told Andy.

Part of me was glad that Jake found all of this out, for Andy's sake, of course. However, another part of me was disappointed, on account that the only way Jake could've gotten the information from Andy's mom, was to tell her what we were doing, and I considered that betrayal. If I would've known he was gonna tell her everything, I would never have asked for his help in the first place.

"How could you, Jake?"

"Could've what?"

"Tell her what we told you, what we were doing!"

"Calm down, little bro, I didn't tell her."

"You didn't? Then what were you two talking about in the coffee shop, and why did you leave your keys on the table?"

After hurtling more questions at Jake, I looked around to see the boys on my side, all looking at Jake for his answers. All except Andy, who just stared blankly out the window.

Jake told us that Andy's mom was quite nice and friendly, and that they just went for a drive. He never answered my questions, and I couldn't tell if he was telling us the whole truth. I also wasn't so sure about the boys, who seemed kinda disappointed that she wasn't an escort after all, despite the fact that she was still Andy's mom. Jake said that she was stressed out, and needed to talk to someone.

"Come on, big brother, since when does a woman just meet a guy and then go for a drive, just cause she's stressed out?"

"It wasn't like that, little man, but you'll understand when you're older."

"Oh, gimmie a break. Save the 'you'll understand when you're older' crap, for somebody else!"

"What is it that you want to hear?"

"Did you tell her who you were, your real name?"

"Yes and no."

Over the years, I'd learned that a 'yes and no' response was the mark of a good question. When you could get a grown-up to answer 'yes' and 'no' to a question, then that meant that the truth was likely to follow. Like the old saying, 'I've got good news, and I've got bad news'.

Jake went on to tell us that he used his first name only and that he never told her about us. He said that she told him that she didn't feel like a good person, neither a good wife nor mother, and that she was actually sad at the way her life turned out. He told us that she only mentioned Andy once or twice, and didn't go into much detail about him except that he was always with his friends and always seemed happy. The part about us was true, but not about Andy being happy, except when he was with us, which she didn't ever get to see.

Jake told us that it would be better if we didn't say anything to Andy's parents about him, on account that he didn't want to blow our cover. We agreed and decided to get out of the car.

"What are you guys gonna do, you want me to wait for you, little bro?"

"No, that's alright, I think we're gonna take a trip down memory lane, as you adults would say."

"Touché, little bro, touché."

"Got any money, though, so we can get a soda or something to munch on?"

"No, sorry, those coffees took my last dime."

# BOYS WILL BE BOYS

Jake didn't know it at the time, but I had just tested him. Thank goodness, the boys hadn't caught on either, except Jack, of course, who caught most things people thought he couldn't. Jack didn't have to ask what I was thinking, but confirmed that he knew, when he whispered to me (as Jake drove away), so the others didn't hear him.

"I don't believe him, either. Didn't he just get paid yesterday?"

"Yea, Jack, he did."

I had the awful feeling, right then and there, that Andy's mom was actually an escort, and that Jake wasn't telling the whole truth. I figured that Jake did spend his last dime on coffee, but that he spent all his others on a date with Andy's mom. Me and Jack quickly caught up to the boys and he went to Andy's left side, while I hung behind the group.

Greenfield Avenue ran east to west and Jake had brought us to the west side, which meant that we'd be walking east, towards the rising sun. Staying up late and functioning on little to no sleep usually wasn't an issue for any of us, let alone any kid. It was just that we were all emotionally drained, or at least I was. We all had energy, but I think we just needed closure. Then again, maybe I just think too much. Which, of course, would throw off just about every argument a parent could throw at a kid, on account that it's not that we don't think, but that we probably thought too much.

We stopped in old man Wilson's store, to get in from the brisk air for a moment, and hoped that it was Mrs. Wilson that was working. To our dismay, it was Mr. Wilson who was working. None of us knew if he had recognized Jack or not, but we formed a semi-circle around him and weren't going to ask Mr. Wilson anything.

We left as soon as we warmed up some. Even though the sun was out and the sky was clear, late winters and early springs here could be brutal at times, and today was no exception. But, we were boys who had snowball fights without gloves on and jumped through mud puddles, so we could handle a little cold weather. We decided that it would be best if we didn't stop by the butcher shop where Jake said Andy's dad worked, and instead decided to visit the card shop.

Mark thought it would be best if we went around the back of the butcher shop, on account that the card shop was two stores past it, and that we shouldn't take the chance of Andy's dad spotting us. We all agreed and started around towards the back. We were soldiers crossing the enemy line. Like Sgt. Slaughter searching out Cobra, as was clear when Mark yelled for us to hurry up and shouted, "Go, Joe!"

"Now you know, and knowing is half the battle." Brad jokingly responded to Mark, receiving laughs from all of us except Andy.

"Andy, come on now, you know that was funny."

When we heard Brad trying to convince Andy that his timing was perfect, we all knew something was wrong, cause

Andy would've for sure thought that was funny. After all, Brad got that from Andy, on account that Andy used to make fun of the last part of every 'G.I. Joe' episode, when one of the Joes would help kids make the right decisions instead of the wrong ones in certain situations. For instance, one of the Joes would help a kid learn the lesson of not telling strangers where you live, or that you are home alone. After the Joe helped the kid, they would always say, "Now you know, and knowing is half the battle." Andy used to make fun of that and He-Man and his "By the power of Grayskull, I have the power!" routine, but that is another story altogether.

A round of "Where's Andy," followed, by each of the boys. While we were all looking at each other, like we just lost our dog or something, Jack pointed to the front of the butcher shop. Andy was just standing there in the open doorway of the shop. There he was, just standing there, staring blankly inside like a lost puppy who forgot his way home would. And, in that moment, I was almost overcome with sadness, cause here was our friend, a skinny kid who felt

he wasn't loved by his parents, attempting to make a stand.

We had a choice to make and not much time to make

it. Either we could wait for him, here outside, or we could go

in with him and support him. So, once again, I picked my

head up, only to see that the boys were all looking at me like I

was Sgt. Slaughter himself, leading them into battle.

Since the boys left me no options, other than to make

the decision for all of us that could have a serious affect on

our friend. I cleared my throat as quickly as I could, after

playing the two scenarios out in my mind, and told the boys

my decision.

"Jack."

"Yea, boss."

The whole boss thing he got from his stay in Juvenile

Hall after beating his dad with his favorite Louisville Slugger.

He told us that 'boss' was what he and the other inmates

called the guards. He said they were cool enough, that they

treated him like an adult and simply enforced the rules. But, they also talked with him and the others about life choices and consequences. He said that he learned a lot by watching and listening to them.

So, whenever Jack is told by one of us to help out or to do something, he calls us 'boss'. We don't mind either, on account that it sounds all official like. Not that any of us was his real boss or anything, though, but we all knew that we were all he really had in this world.

"Jack, go and get Andy. Mark, stay with me. Paul, you and Brad run past Andy, and into the store. Run hard and run fast, so you're out of breath once you get inside. When Andy's dad or another butcher sees you, tell them that you two were racing and get a look around, and see if you can see Andy's dad, if he's not the one who stops you.

"Hopefully, Andy ain't been standing there this whole time and they haven't seen him yet. Jack, bring him back over here by me and Mark. Brad, you Paul and meet us round back. That's where we'll take him for debriefing. If Andy's gonna do this, then he's not gonna be alone. Me and Mark will have a plan ready when we all meet. Everybody understand?"

And, as if I didn't know what was coming, a round of "yea, boss" followed and then a quick round of laughs. Well Jack didn't laugh, but the rest of us did.

The boys did a good job and Andy was with them when they got back to me and Mark. The plan we came up with was to have only one of us go back with Andy; if that's what he wanted to do. We knew adults well enough to know that if they got cornered, just like a cat, they would get defensive and then nothing good would be accomplished. Me and Mark decided that Brad should go with, since he was the most mature one out of us all.

Me and the rest of the boys knew that Jack couldn't go with Andy, on account that he might beat up Andy's dad or something. We decided that the rest of us should go and wait in the card shop until Brad and Andy got back.

None of that whole plan even mattered though, cause Andy had snapped out of his daze and told us that he didn't want to talk to his dad. He said he just wanted to see if what Jake told us was true. It was true, it turned out, cause Andy saw his dad and his dad saw him.

We decided to ditch our plan of walking down memory lane, and started the walk home. Jack came home with me, and the rest of the boys went to their house's, including Andy. It was the first time we had walked home from Greenfield Avenue together, where no one talked to each other.

# BOYS WILL BE BOYS

## Jimmy
## Summer 1991

Jimmy wasn't like any other kid we'd ever known, but we all were kinda thankful for that in a way. Mom used to tell me and the boys that if we didn't have anything nice to say about other people, then we shouldn't say anything at all. And, it was a good thing that we all listened to her, cause when we first saw Jimmy, we didn't say a word.

Kids, generally, had a tough time concealing how they felt, on account that it was always written on their faces. There weren't actual words on their foreheads or anything; it was just an expression that adults used when telling a kid that they could tell what they were thinking about, by the looks on their faces.

However, for kids like Brad and me, we could read what adults were thinking, using their own trick. And, you know what? We found out really quickly that adults not only lie more than kids do, but they hide their feelings more than kids do, too.

It was in the spring when we first met Jimmy and his sister, Cindy. We had seen them move into the old Whitaker place, off Washington Street, which was down the block and the street to the right from my house. We were all playing baseball at La Follette Park, the closest park to the neighborhood, when Jimmy and his sister showed up.

We used to play 'strike out' at the grade school, but when we got older we figured that we'd better play at the park, on account that we threw harder, ran faster, and hit deeper. Strike out used to be perfect for us, cause you really only needed three kids for it; one pitcher, one batter, and one fielder. You drew on a concrete or brick wall, in chalk, a large square about three feet up from the ground and it served as the 'Strike Zone'. The fielder went out and waited for the batter to hit and the pitcher tried to strike out the batter. When the batter struck out, the players rotated.

# BOYS WILL BE BOYS

Without enough kids for a full team, me and the boys mostly played '500', or 'catch', or 'pickle'. '500' was a pretty cool game, but catch was my favorite, on account that you could talk with the kid you were playing with. You could throw a pitch, like a fastball or work on a curve ball, or throw a 'pop-up', a grounder, or a line drive. You could pretend you were in warm-ups, right in the outfield at County Stadium, next to Robin Yount. Well, at least, that's what I always did.

'500' was when you had one batter and everyone else was in the outfield. The batter had all the baseballs at his feet, and the only bat. He'd then toss the ball up to himself, like a tennis player tosses up a lob for his serve, and then the batter would hit a pop-up. Well, he was supposed to hit a pop-up, cause there were times when he'd hit a few grounders and everybody would rag on him to hit it higher. When the ball was hit high enough to be counted, everybody in the outfield would run and try to catch it. When someone caught it, they got '100' and the first person to get to '500', would get to be the batter. We knew that there were other rules and variations of ours, but we liked how we played, so we kept it that way.

'Pickle' was equally as cool as '500', cause it was the classic 'run-down'. You didn't see it that much in the 'majors', only about as much as the infamous 'balk', but it happened enough. A 'run-down' was when a player was in-between bases, and the two infielders tried to tag him out before he reached one of the bases safely. You'd pick two markers as bases; we usually used trees, and three people. Whoever ended up tagging the runner out would then be the runner, and the runner would then be the infielder.

We were playing '500' when Jimmy and his sister showed up. It was easy talking about a kid when he wasn't there to hear it, but it was another thing altogether when the kid was around. When Jimmy and his sister showed up, I was batting and the boys came in after they saw that I had stopped hitting. None of them spoke as they ran in, but their eyes were certainly glued on Jimmy. Just like always, the boys stood in a semi-circle behind me, as we faced Jimmy and his sister.

I don't know if the boys were staring at Jimmy or not, but I was looking at his sister. I soon felt one of the boys tugging on my shirt and figured they wanted me to say something. To 'break the ice', as adults would say when they were nervous about meeting others and someone had to make the first move; to say something first. So, I took the boys cue and ran with it.

"You guys the ones who moved into the old Whitaker place on Washington Street?"

"Yea, we are," Jimmy's sister answered, as she moved closer to us and in front of her brother.

She only said a few words, but I wondered right there if it was possible to fall in love at first sight. We never really had any experience with girls; never even thought of them in any love kinda way, but I had watched Jake a lot and learned a few things along the way. Like how to treat them like queens,

119

look them in their eyes when you talked to them, and listen to what they have to say.

"I'm Cindy, and this is my brother, Jimmy."

Her voice was like the church choir and I felt my mouth open as if I was going to introduce myself, but nothing came out. I soon felt one of the boys tug at my shirt again. I cleared my throat, turned sideways, and started from my right.

"That's Jack, Brad, Andy, Paul, Mark, and I'm Joey."

"Well, it's nice to meet you all," the choir sang again.

Cindy looked older than we did; I guessed that she was about 15 years old, and wondered if she had a boyfriend. In the midst of the silence that fell around us, I couldn't figure out why I was having these thoughts. After all, she was just a girl, not unlike any others that I knew. On account of my thoughts briefly taking control of me, I couldn't figure out why I felt so protective over her. I think that I was starting to have an instant 'crush' on her.

BOYS WILL BE BOYS

The 'crush', an infamous term used by kids to identify those thoughts and feelings about girls that they didn't understand. Now, I'm sure that girls got crushes on boys too, but girls were much better at not telling secrets. And, barring any real life issues, crushes were about the biggest secrets kids had.

It always amazed me how fast the human mind operated, on account that I could have like a hundred different thoughts in only a matter of seconds. So, I cleared my throat again and spoke. This time, I looked Cindy in her eyes, which was easy, on account that she was close to my height.

"Does your brother talk?"

The second the words left my mouth, I wanted to take them back, even though by hearing the boys exhale, I knew I was speaking for them. It was borderline not nice, but us kids could get away with that from time to time, on account that we hadn't mastered the adult practice of saying one thing and meaning another.

"Yea, I can talk! And, I can hit too! I might not look like you all do; not that what I'm looking at is all that special!"

"Jimmy Allen, you apologize now!"

It seemed as though the choir was like his mother or something, as was evident by the boys all snickering behind me. That's what kids do; they snicker and laugh when another kid gets yelled at in front of them.

"No, let's just go home, Cindy, I didn't think they could play anyway."

Just as Cindy took a step back and was even with her brother, put her arm around him, and started to leave, she said sorry to us all. However, right at that moment, we all heard something that didn't surprise any of us, but did catch us off guard.

"Can you put your money where your mouth is? You say you can hit, but I say prove it, cause we boys don't talk about things we can't do!"

I didn't have to look to know that it was Jack who was now standing next to me.

"Anytime, anywhere, big man!" Jimmy limped in front of his sister, as he called Jack out.

It didn't surprise us, what Jack did, cause we all knew he had the biggest heart of any kid in these United States of America. He wasn't as good as me and Brad at reading the faces of adults, but he was probably the best at reading the faces of kids. Jack had it rough, we all knew, and just by looking at Jimmy, we knew that he must've had it rough too.

We all knew what Jack was doing, cause he was Jack, and he was one of us; one of the boys. He was showing Jimmy respect, in the only way a kid could, by giving him an opportunity to prove himself. We all knew it wasn't right;

how the world sometimes worked, but we also knew that we had to live in it and therefore play by its rules.

Some might call it competition, but us kids know it better as nature, on account that we are born with this need to prove ourselves to each other. In science class, they taught us that we are part of an evolutionary chain, like we grow out of our past. And, just like us boys, when people are forced to live with other people, there has to be a way in which we all decide who we want to be around the most.

It wasn't that Jack felt sorry for Jimmy, though none of us would've blamed him if he did, it was more like Jack was challenging him and by doing so, he was letting the kid know that he didn't feel sorry for him. He was giving him the opportunity to prove that we shouldn't feel sorry for him. Everybody liked attention; moms, dads, brothers, sisters, friends, and especially kids, as it's what drives us and helps us become who we are.

# BOYS WILL BE BOYS

However, it is tricky to balance the amount of attention and the origin of it. The kids that got too much attention were called 'mamma's boys' or 'sissy's', and those who didn't get enough usually got the pity. The feeling of being loved and belonging was just about the best feeling a kid could have. It was pity that people tried to stay away from, cause that's like feeling sorry for someone, times a million. So, as much as a kid likes attention, he doesn't so much like being felt sorry for, and none of us knew that more than Jack. We then, by keeping quiet, let him ride this thing out.

"The game's called 'Strike Out'."

Jack told Jimmy the name of the game he was challenging him to, and handed him the bat we were playing with. They didn't say a word to each other as we walked to our old grade school. We knew that Jack was aware of Jimmy's limp, cause a kid would have to be blind not to notice. Jack walked slow, but not so slow as to make it a tough walk for this kid who issued a 'call out' to the biggest kid in the neighborhood.

Cindy walked with me, behind Jack and Jimmy and in front of the rest of the boys. She told me that she was getting worried about her little brother, on account that Jimmy was breathing so hard that we could hear it from behind them. I told her not to sweat it too much, cause Jack knew what he was doing.

"I've got to see this. Jack's gonna cream this kid!"

Cindy turned around, but I didn't need to cause I knew the boys were just being the boys. We were all used to getting up for games, motivating each other to do better. Cindy wasn't used to it and that's why she turned around. It didn't surprise me at all when, the moment she turned around, the boys stopped dead in their tracks and were as quiet as church mice. That's what mom used to tell me when she needed me to be really quiet.

# BOYS WILL BE BOYS

However comical it was to hear the boys getting pumped up, my smile was met with a choir gone mad.

"That's funny to you; your friends back there saying that your friend Jack is gonna cream my little brother?"

"That's why I smiled, cause their the boys and that's what they do. Hopefully, you'll understand what I mean, but you got to get to know us first."

"Is he gonna hurt Jimmy, cause if he is, you'd better tell me now!"

"Why are you so protective of him, anyway? The way I see it; anybody that can call out Jack, who is by far the biggest and toughest kid in the neighborhood, I would think wouldn't need his big sister protecting him."

I made sure not to ask anything about Jimmy directly, cause I was a kid and I know kids, and I knew that if Jimmy wanted to, he'd tell us himself what happened to him.

"Aren't you a bit young to be a jerk?"

"Now, I know why I like you."

"What?"

"Ahhh…nothing, what I meant was that if Jimmy is anything like his big sister, he'll be just fine."

However, what I was thinking was that I couldn't believe that I just said that.

"Kids can be brutal, Cindy, but they're honest for the most part, and not one single one of us here, would purposely hurt anyone who hasn't hurt us first. We don't operate like that. Boys can be brutal, and girls can be mean and break hearts, and that's life. We boys are tight and we've been through a lot, and we're still together, and that means something to all of us."

"I didn't mean it like that. It's just…I was just saying that…"

"It's okay, us boys, we don't do excuses. You said it cause you were mad and you probably meant it to hurt me, but don't take it back. You were scared; heck, I'd be scared if I didn't know Jack so well. Jack's a big kid, but I'll tell you

128

what, you could go around and ask any one of us who had the softest heart, and they'd all tell you that Jack does."

"You're kind of deep for a kid. Are all you guys, I mean the boys, all this deep?"

"Like I said, Cindy, we've been through a lot and we're still together. You'll see, if you want to."

The school was a good ten-minute walk from La Follette Park and whether I wanted to believe my eyes or not, Jimmy was making it just fine. When we reached the school, Jack and Jimmy went straight to the strike out wall and the boys all went to the outfield. While Cindy and me watched from the side, Jimmy spoke up.

"I'm thinking you guys might want to back up and fan yourselves out, unless you all want to chase balls."

I expected the boys to laugh and maybe even make a few jokes, but to my surprise, they didn't say a word. Instead, they did just as Jimmy suggested and fanned out across the outfield, which was really the playground's kickball diamond.

129

Cindy hadn't let go of my arm, and pulled me off the field and next to the fence, to the left of where Jack was gonna pitch.

It was silent when Jimmy walked to the chalk outline of the strike zone, into the invisible batter's box, and hit the bat against the wall. I couldn't hear the birds or any cars; it was completely quiet, leaving my own voice in my head as the only sounds I heard. I didn't notice that Cindy was holding on to my hand until it started to hurt, on account that she was squeezing the crap out of it. She probably thought Jack was gonna take her brother's head off, and she needed something to hold onto. In a weird kinda way, I was glad I was there for her.

The second I saw the ball leave Jack's hand, my sound came back. And, it was just in time to hear the crack of the bat breaking in half, as Jimmy swung for the fences. Cindy let go of my hand and was clapping and cheering, and when I looked up, I saw why. At first, I saw the ball flying high in the

130

air and then I caught the look on Mark's face, and I thought for a moment that his eyes were gonna pop out of his head.

Jimmy hit Jack's pitch over all the boys' heads, and cleared the fence beyond the basketball court. The ball hit the side of the big purple house behind the boys. I went around the fence to look for it, and Cindy followed me.

When Cindy and me got back, we saw that the boys were all standing around Jimmy, and giving him high fives. Cindy was so happy that she turned and smiled at me, and I heard the choir again; this time they were singing, "thank you."

# Jeremy Aldana

## Bobby
## Fall 1991

Bobby was what you might call 'distant', but he was still my brother. He liked to read a lot, and was apparently good at it, cause all those D & D books were mega-long. If anyone ever wanted to find Bobby, chances were that he had his nose buried in some 600 page book. I never knew what it was that drew him into those stories; into those worlds, but whatever it was had quite a grip on him. I had my baseball, football, and basketball cards; Jake had his expensive shoes and clothes, and Bobby had his stories.

Bobby was the middle kid, the so-called forgotten one of the family. I'm not sure who ever said, so-called, but I bet they never met Paul, on account that he wasn't the middle kid and he was surely forgotten about. Despite Paul not being the middle child and still being forgotten about, I think that they were right about the so-called thing, cause I can look back now, and sort of see how Bobby was sometimes forgotten about. I'm not sure if he minded his assigned role, but he certainly adapted well to it.

Me and Jake always joked with mom and told her that we knew that Bobby was her favorite. She always denied it, but we knew. We also knew that it was okay, on account that it was her way to let Bobby know that he was always loved. If there was one thing I learned from her, though I learned a lot, that stuck with me the most; it was that she always loved us, and always let us know that we were loved.

Her message was not only received by me, Jake, and Bobby, but by the boys as well. With Brad's gracefulness and mom's words on my tongue, we made sure that the boys understood it perfectly.

Ever since the accident happened, I hadn't talked about Bobby, and this is the first time I really thought about him. Was that wrong? It wasn't like I wanted to talk about the accident or about him, I just missed my brother.

Speaking of missing my brother, and remembering the accident, I just had a thought about Dr. Ron and how the boys grew to not care much for him. They knew that I didn't have much of a choice about going to see him though, and didn't give me too much grief, to which I'm glad. They all wanted assurances that I wasn't going to tell him about them and their 'messed up' lives, as they put it. I told them that we were boys and they could trust me, and that should've been enough.

The boys, for sure, would've had me 'tarred and feathered' if they would've ever found out that sometimes I did talk about them. Dr. Ron told me not to worry, on account of some 'patient-doctor confidentiality rule' or something. I didn't tell him everything about the boys, only bits and pieces, here and there, but I must've told him enough. He said that it was obvious that the boys meant the world to me. That was all too true, cause they did; we were boys, and not even he could change that.

# BOYS WILL BE BOYS

Ever since that day, when Jimmy belted that towering shot over the fences, he and Cindy were kinda liked welcomed around. She told us that their parents moved them here from Pennsylvania, after Jimmy's accident, to get a fresh start. It wasn't so much a new start so far as Cindy saw it, she said, but more like a change of scenery.

It didn't take long, not as long as the boys predicted it would anyway, for Jimmy to open up and tell us what happened to him. We weren't morbid or nothing; we didn't chase fire trucks or ambulances, or anything like that, we were just curious about this kid. Brad made us promise not to say anything or even ask him about it, despite his obvious limp. He was a little kid by all accounts. He was shorter than all of us, but swore he was our age, and Cindy was there to confirm it.

# Jeremy Aldana

## The Invisible Line
## Fall 1991

We were all blown away when Jimmy told us. I think he knew he had our attention too, cause he didn't skip a beat when he told us. He even allowed us to ask him questions when he was done. He seemed so detached from it, like it had happened to someone else. I guess that was his way of dealing with it.

When a kid gets hurt, it's kinda like a 'rite of passage'. Something like, "Well, I broke my arm climbing a tree," or "I broke my leg sliding into second." Most kids are like that, you know, their proud of their wounds. It's their way of being tough or looking like their tough. Sure, most kids cried but they did that at home where someone was there to console them, make them feel better, and let them know that it was okay to cry.

For kids like Jack, who had nobody there for them, they didn't get to cry; they didn't let themselves cry, cause they learned that crying was a weakness. The tears would become a sign of weakness and since they didn't have them, they learned to tell themselves that they were the opposite of weak, tough. And, toughness was a trait that boys learned was a necessity in order to become men.

I learned that tears come from pain, but I also know that pain comes from the mind and if you choose not to feel the pain, whether physical or emotional, then there is no pain. At least not any that is apparent to anyone that's watching. What's really tough is letting yourself feel the pain, and telling yourself that it's okay to do so. That lesson I learned the hard way, but it's one that I will always try to share with the boys and anyone else I know that's in pain.

It was rare, for us boys anyway, to see a kid so detached and not proud of his wounds like Jimmy was. I had a theory, one that came to me even as Jimmy told us what happened to him. There was, there had to be, like an invisible line somewhere that was either crossed or wasn't.

# Jeremy Aldana

On one side of the line was the norm; the everyday things, the bumps, the bruises, and the roadblocks, where most people stayed. Where, if you were behind it and hadn't crossed it, it was safe because it was where most people were, as there was safety in numbers. It was where most had experienced everything that you had or were going through. It was safe, cause people understood and that made one heck of a difference. When someone else has gone through what you were going through and they told you that you were gonna make it through, like they did, you feel a little comfort.

It was on the other side of that invisible line, where there was no going back. Where there was no certainty of peace, and lots of pain to deal with. I can only see that invisible line, on account that I crossed it. It was more like someone pushed me over it though, cause I would've never voluntarily crossed it. And, I can tell you now, that once you've crossed it, you can't go back and stay on the other side. And, then the closer you look ahead of you, the more

138

lines you see. More lines that you fear crossing and end up hoping that someone will push you across them again, cause the fear holds you back.

It was on the other side of that line where only a few were proud of their wounds, of what they went through and chances were that their pride was only a mask. At least that's how I see it, cause I certainly ain't proud of what I've had to go through. I would trade my wound for anything in the world. I would give everything up just to go back on the other side of that line, where it was safe. And, no doubt, the boys would too.

We boys are measured by our toughness, well into our manhood and beyond. And, if anyone was to know us boys, they'd know in a heartbeat that we were among the tough ones. With that toughness comes respect, whether it's from another's fear or from admiration. There was no doubt that we respected Jimmy, if not from the monster shot over the fences, then from his story.

In a way, I just knew that Jimmy's lack of ownership for what happened to him was just his way of dealing with it. And, of course, he got my respect because of it.

# BOYS WILL BE BOYS

## The Accident
## Fall 1991

Dr. Ron told me that I think too much, and of course, I thought about that. He was right though, and it was confirmed each time someone told me I was too deep for them. What does that mean, anyway? I know that people can meditate, do yoga, and clear their minds and all that, but I could never seem to find the time. Me and the boys just wanted to be kids, for as long as I can remember. We just wanted to be regular teenagers, but things always seemed to come up, things that we had to deal with. Dr. Ron said that it was okay to let loose sometimes, and make time for being a kid. When I told him a funny story about one weekend we had, where we were having fun and being kids again, he said that 'boys will be boys', and that was okay.

It's hard for me, just like the boys, to not think about things so much. It wasn't like we were sweating about the latest pair of Air Jordan's or anything like that. We sweated about where we were gonna sleep, how we were gonna help each other get out of some jam, and stuff like that. He was right, when he told me that if any one of us had to deal with our problems alone, then we'd probably go crazy. How that translated to me was, I then knew why so many kids killed themselves.

Suicide was bad, cause it meant death and dying, and never coming back. Most grown-ups we knew didn't like the subject, and no one ever talked to us about it; not one time. We boys did think about it though, on account that most kids did at some point in their lives. We talked about suicide in general, never personally, and decided that it was not the way to go out, especially since we had each other. And, was I ever glad that none of us had ever tried it, cause we boys were committed. We finished what we started, and never gave up. Suicide was the line that ended all lines.

As Jimmy was finishing up, telling us about his accident, I noticed out of the corner of my eye that Cindy was crying. When Jimmy called us to the park that morning, he had been alone. She must've showed up while Jimmy had our attention. I don't think any of the boys even noticed her, on account they hadn't taken their eyes off of Jimmy. And, as we sat 'cross-legged' in a semi-circle watching and listening to Jimmy use hand gestures and medical terms, I suddenly felt the wetness of the grass under me.

It was like I snapped out of a trance or something, and when I looked up towards Jimmy, our eyes met for a second. In that moment, when our eyes met, he had motioned me over to his sister who was behind Jack, to my left, next to Brad. For a second, I didn't know what to do. I didn't know if he really motioned me to his sister, or if my mind was playing a trick on me. It wasn't that my mind was always playing tricks on me; it was just that I knew I liked her. I knew that I had a crush on her, even though I didn't tell any of the boys, and even tried telling myself that I didn't. In that second, I wondered if I just wanted to be next to her.

Either way, whether Jimmy actually motioned me to her or whether I just wanted a reason to be by her; I knew that the only real important thing was that she not be alone. It must have been tough for her to have her little brother go through so much suffering, and to have to be there because he needed her to be. And, now, here she was reliving the whole ordeal for the benefit of us boys. Seeing now, how Cindy was reacting to Jimmy's story made me think that maybe the reason he showed no attachment to his accident, was cause she took his burdens for him.

It also dawned on me that there might have been something else that Jimmy wasn't telling us, on account of Cindy's strong emotional reaction. I got the feeling that his accident left him with more than just a limp, but I was never gonna ask. That was something for him to share on his own.

# BOYS WILL BE BOYS

## Cindy
## Fall 1991

Cindy and Jimmy, before they moved by us in the Midwest, told us that they grew up in Philly. Seeing as how Jimmy could talk about the Eagles and the Phillies for hours on end, we probably would have been able to figure it out in the long run.

Cindy told me that she used to go to downtown Philly, to go to the mall with her friends a couple times a month. She said she loved the mall, on account that there were so many different people there to meet. She told me that she never really had any 'real' boyfriends, but only guys she would meet at the mall when she went. You have to understand, I only know all this stuff cause she told me so, and as far as me remembering it, well I couldn't tell you how.

I never told the boys all the things that me and Cindy talked about, but instead just a few of the highlights every now and then. I think I never fully let them on to what I was

145

always doing with her, cause I didn't want them to get jealous. I know they wouldn't have ever stepped in on my crush or anything, but I also kinda liked being able to tell things in a way that made me seem a lot smoother than I really was.

Cindy was cool though, on account that she knew that the boys and I were family and that they came first. Besides, when she wasn't around, I got to embellish just a bit on my stories about stuff we did and talked about. It was like I had this invisible story-tellers license that allowed me make it up as I went, if I needed to. Or, I could add a detail or subtract two, if the story called for it. It was all about the audience; how they reacted to it, and to you. Writers and poets use some invisible license to create their works, and I guess it's sort of like that.

I only say invisible, on account that it's not a certificate you can frame or anything, but instead it's just a way to think and relate ideas. You know, so they are original even if they are made up. And, besides all that, I was a boy

146

and that's what teenage boys did when they talked about their crushes.

It wasn't, in the beginning anyway, a mutual acceptance of ideas or arrangements between Cindy and me. I was good at hiding my crush from her for a while, or at least that's what I always thought. Jack was the one who burst my bubble, when he told me in front of the boys that she knew about me crushing on her. Of course, backed into a corner and getting defensive, on account of my embarrassment, I came back with the cliché comeback of every teenage boy who just had been called out on his crush. I grinned and smirked at Jack and said, "Yea, well, you're just jealous!"

Jack wasn't jealous, and me and the boys all knew it too. I was busted and after they all laughed, snorted, and pointed at me, they told me that it was cool. They were actually proud of me, they said, for having a crush on an older girl, let alone a girl that was actually cool enough to hang out with. I took the semi-compliments slash semi-admiration, and grinned from ear to ear. Bobby and Jake

would have said that I was blushing and I would've accepted

that, if it meant I got to see them again.

Cindy was cool though, cause she never changed

when we hung out, despite knowing that I liked her. She

never really talked about it with me, but she never told me to

'get lost' either, which is usually what happened when one of

us tried to go out with one of them. She always smelled good

and always had her pretty hair curled and brushed. She even

would shoot me a smile from across the room, every now and

then. She never out right said it, but I kinda think that she

liked all the extra attention I gave her.

She was always concerned about Jimmy, even though

he would always tell her that he was okay. She worried a lot

about him and told us boys, during one of the few occasions

when he wasn't with us, how much she appreciated us

hanging out with him, on account that he was so happy when

he was with us.

# BOYS WILL BE BOYS

Shock, I guess you could say is what happened to Cindy that day she thanked us for the charity we gave to her brother. As if the blank, wide-eyed stare or the jaw-dropping gasp didn't give her reaction away, then the tears did the job just fine. She was shocked by our reaction, and had no clue as to just how much she offended us. We told her, in a not so nice and affectionate way, that her time was up for that day. We informed her, with some of Webster's finest four letter words they left out of their dictionary, that her speech was over and then we thanked her for her time and showed her the front door.

She was crying when she left my house that afternoon, and then again later that week when she came back to talk to me, after the boys had gone home. She told me that she had no idea that she was offending us. All she meant, she said, was that she was really glad that Jimmy had some good friends. She said that she wasn't mad at me and the boys at all, not now that she knew how she insulted us.

What we boys told her was that we didn't give pity or charity to anyone, let alone her brother. Jimmy could've definitely qualified for some pity, but neither us nor him wanted any of it. We basically told her that we hung with her and Jimmy cause we liked them, not cause Jimmy's got health stuff going on. We told her that Jimmy was cool and a lot stronger, and more together than she gave him credit for.

Cindy later told me that she knew Jimmy was tough, but she felt a certain need to look after him. She told me that she felt responsible for him, and not just as a big sister looking after her brother. It was then that she started to cry and stopped talking altogether.

# BOYS WILL BE BOYS

## The Bases
## Fall 1991

Cindy was a good big sister, as far as any of us could tell, and we talked about it too. She'd come and play '500' with us and even camped out with us a couple of times. And, even though she said that she was doing it on account of Jimmy, for his benefit, we could tell that she had fun. She was warming up to us, not as quickly as Jimmy did, but quick enough just the same.

I always figured she held back some, cause she was a girl in a group of boys. She wasn't a 'tomboy' or nothing, but we could tell she liked hanging out with us. Part of me still thinks it was because we remembered how to be kids, even though the world was forcing us to grow up. I think that she grew up a lot while she took care of Jimmy, and that's why she always had a blast when we hung out. By the way, did you know that choirs had the sweetest laughs?

None of us boys had ever spent as much time with a girl as we did with Cindy. Brad's older sister was the only comparison we had, and she was long gone by now. We'd ask Cindy all sorts of questions about girls, only on account that we were all teenagers and she was a great resource for us. In fact, she'd say that we were all cute when we asked her stuff about girls, crushes, and things. Now, none of us had ever (I mean ever!) been known to be shy in anyway, but when we talked about other girls with her, we did have our moments of weakness. A few times, I caught some of the boys blushing when Cindy called them out on their crushes. Yea, she definitely fit in after a while. If you could make big ole' Jack blush and turn scarlet red then you had a place with us.

Sure, I had a crush on Cindy, did from the first moment I saw her; all the dramatics of a teenage boy included. Usually when the girl getting crushed on is older than the boy crushing on her, it meant that the boy never stood a chance. What could I do though, what kid my age wouldn't have a crush on her? She had strawberry blonde

hair, at least that's what she called it, but it just looked to me

like reddish-yellow. Her hair was long, down towards the

middle of her back and it was always curly at the ends, and

looked really soft. I used to think that she'd made up the

'strawberry blonde' color, cause her hair always smelled so

sweet to me. She had these blue eyes that were the color of

those lakes that were near the mountains. I'd never seen the

lakes in person mind you, but only in pictures in magazines

like the National Geographic.

Now, if you were to have asked me what I meant,

when I first thought that eye-lake thing, I would've told you

that I had no idea, on account that I was crushing on her.

When boys crush on girls, sometimes they say stupid things

like that and then hope that the girl takes a compliment out

of it. Seriously, though, whenever I looked into her eyes,

those mountain lakes were the pictures that popped into my

mind, kinda like in the background.

Jeremy Aldana

She also had an older girl's body, complete with bras and everything. We knew a little about bras, on account that our moms had them and Brad's sister had them. We had an idea about them, but not much real information. All we knew was what we had heard from Jake and Bobby, and the movies, of course. We knew that we were supposed to be able to take them off a girl when we would reach a certain base on the baseball diamond.

The 'infamous' bases were a rite of passage for every teenage boy, and we were no different. We all knew about them, and those who didn't probably weren't supposed to, thus they probably wouldn't reach them until their wedding night. None of us had ever even been up to the plate to get a chance to bat, let alone make it to first or second base.

It was widely known, accepted, and expected that by the time a kid started his freshman year that he'd, at the very least, would've reached first base. By the end of their freshman year, they were expected to reach second base.

Junior year and senior year followed with more goals like those ones. It was a part of growing up as a boy; we really had no choice, people were counting on us.

I never thought about any of those things when I was around Cindy, only on account that I had to fight off my nerves just to remain myself. Of course, I wanted to impress her and show her that I was mature for my age, and not just cute, cause no kid our age liked being in the 'cute' category. It usually meant that they were just going to be friends. I didn't know if Cindy thought I was cute or not, but I desperately hoped she didn't.

Girls like Cindy didn't date guys that were cute, but dated 'good looking' guys. So, there you go, I had less than a school year to go from being a 'boy' to being a 'guy'. And, I would also have to make that leap from being cute to good looking; that is if Cindy thought I was cute in the first place, which I hope she hadn't.

I'm still not sure who learned more from each other about the opposite sexes (that's what adults called men and women, when they compared them), us about girls or Cindy about boys. We learned that girls were much cooler than we ever thought. Like how we learned not to be so scared around them as much, on account that Cindy helped us understand that they were still kids too. They were growing up just like we were, only different.

Do you see now, why girls are so hard to understand? None of us fully understand how the same could be different, but we accepted it the best we could. And, she learned that boys were always trying to have fun doing whatever it was that they were doing. She also got to see how loyal we were to each other; how we were always there for each other, no matter what. That was one way we were different, she told us, on account that girls weren't always like that. Like how sometimes they were more concerned with how people saw them, and thought about them, as in how they looked or who they hung out with. To that, me and the boys gave her a collective, "Ahhh…"

We didn't have too much of a clue as to what she said a bunch of times, but we got good practice at acting not only interested in what a girl was saying, but also making them believe that we totally understood their points.

# Jeremy Aldana

## The NES
## Fall 1991

Cindy and Jimmy must've had a Nintendo back in Philly, cause they put us all to shame on a few of our own games. Jimmy mastered 'Mega Man', and didn't even need the coveted code to 'Contra' to beat the game. Any kid, who has ever played 'Contra', will forever remember the code. It was a milestone for video games, and for us kids. It was a hidden code, a secret code that only those who played knew. If you did it right, then you were unstoppable.

Cindy was the only one of us who could ever beat Tyson on 'Mike Tyson's Punch-Out!' which was only the best boxing game ever. We could all get to Tyson, but always got knocked out. To her credit, she was a girl and that made her so much cooler. I was the master at 'The Legend of Zelda', Brad reigned supreme at 'Super Mario Bros.', Mark was champ at 'Tecmo Bowl, Andy crushed us all at 'Blades of Steel', and Paul was king at 'RC Pro-Am'.

# BOYS WILL BE BOYS

It was Jimmy though, who was the best at 'Baseball Stars', and none of us could come close to hitting as many homeruns as he could. He had a blast with that game, on account that it was the first game ever, which allowed you to create your own player, and use him on your team. I think he liked that game best, cause his player in the game was in perfect health and quite good at baseball too. Video games were a great way for kids to lose themselves in another reality, one where the rules never changed and one where if you died, then chances were that you had another couple of lives to finish the level or game with. You could also just reset the game, and start over with more lives.

We played the NES (Nintendo) at my house, on account that I had a room in the basement, where we had lots of space. The basement was always cool, in the hot and humid summer days Milwaukee was famous for. It was there, in my room, towards the end of the summer when we decided to make it official. We were going to 'induct' Jimmy and Cindy into our group, which was something we didn't take lightly. We all talked several times about it and unanimously voted to invite them, officially in. They were to become the newest members of 'The Boys', which we took to be nothing less than an honor.

It was right after Cindy finally taught Jack how to beat Tyson, that we decided to tell her and Jimmy the good news. I had my little speech prepared (basically I was gonna 'wing it'), and had two fresh copies of handwritten rules that we boys swore to uphold forever. When Jack finished getting his butt handed to him by Tyson, again, I gave the nod to Brad to turn the game off. I thought, for a second, that Jack was gonna pound him until I saw him look up at all our faces, which showed severe disapproval. Then I watched him set the controller down and heard him grunt something about being sorry to Brad, "Oh, yea, I forgot, my bad."

Jack then took his seat in the rocking chair mom left me (it was her mother's), which was one of three chairs in my room. They were strategically placed to the left of my bed, which was a queen size that took up almost a quarter of the space. Brad and me sat on the end of my bed, just like we always did. Mark and Paul sat in their usual places, which were the other two chairs. They were like comfortable recliners that stood on four legs, but didn't recline. Andy sat in the middle of the loveseat, which was like a mini-couch, between Cindy and Jimmy. Normally, the loveseat fit three of us comfortably, unless Jack was sitting there, cause if he was then it only sat two people.

The rocking chair was an 'antique'. That's what mom used to say, anyhow. It was the reason that Jack was respectful enough that I never had to tell him to take it easy while he sat on it. I never thanked him for that, but I think he knew how much I appreciated it. Dr. Ron told me that Jack was probably so easy on it, cause I always trusted him and he never had that kind of trust given to him before.

The two chairs that Mark and Paul sat in were the ones from the living room, upstairs. They were the ones that Bobby and mom always sat in. The loveseat and the bed belonged to Jake. He had turned the basement it into his little apartment, which I always thought was like one of the coolest things ever. Besides, mom's photo albums and Bobby's books, the furniture was all that I kept after they were gone. My aunt and uncle were cool about it, just like they were about most things, including the boys always hanging out in my room.

Once I saw everyone sitting down, I cleared my throat twice and waited a second until I had everyone's attention. It felt like I was back in the sixth grade, standing in front of the class giving a book report on 'Bridge to Terabithia' (which I did, of course). I started out by announcing that I had an announcement, only to hear Paul ask if I came up with that one myself or if I had help. A good, solid round of chuckles followed and I even started to laugh.

# BOYS WILL BE BOYS

I continued though, and walked past Brad and over to the loveseat, which was only a few steps away.

Once I was standing in front of Cindy and Jimmy, who were sitting on the edge of the cushions staring at me, I noticed the boys all stand up and form the usual semi-circle behind me. Cindy and Jimmy looked, for a moment, like they were sitting outside the principal's office, waiting to receive some kinda punishment for something they didn't do. The seriousness of the room left when we all saw Jimmy jab Cindy in the ribs with his elbow and clearly heard what he told her, with the scowl on his face.

"I told you that you should've helped Jack more in beating Tyson!"

It was hilarious and we all busted up laughing, which must've lightened up their moods too, cause they both were laughing hard too. Jack was only laughing a little bit though, on account that he had actually begged Cindy to help him earlier. I guess Jack finally found someone tougher to beat up.

Besides, it was probably better that way, cause it kept him somewhat humble while playing.

When everyone caught their breath, I started again. I quickly recapped the summer's timeline of events and told them that today was the day that they received their invites into our group, officially into 'The Boys'. Cindy looked a bit confused, but Jimmy was smiling from ear to ear. I then handed them each their own copy of the rules, and pointed out the place where they had to sign at the bottom. It was a bit cheesy to have a contract drawn up, but me and the boys operated in trust and that was just the way it was; the way it had to be.

Cindy was onto her second reading when Jimmy reached for a pen on one of the shelves below the TV, on my 'makeshift' entertainment center. He never made it to the pen though, cause Andy pulled him back down onto the loveseat, while telling him, "Not so fast!"

Brad then took over the proceeding, on account that he looked most lawyer-like to us. He started by telling them that they had one week to read the entire rule sheet and memorize it, word for word. He told them, that if they couldn't do that, then they would be denied entrance into the group. He then told them that they were to bring it with them to next week's campout, 'the annual back to school campout', and be ready for initiations.

We really didn't have any initiations but it was Jack's idea to scare them a bit, to which we all agreed without any hesitation. Brad finished by telling them that they must now go, study the rules, and prepare themselves for next week. He told them that celebrations would commence once their induction was official. It was quite dramatic, with Brad's professional and serious tone. Cindy and Jimmy then left, smiling, as they proudly carried their rule sheets upstairs and out of the house.

# Jeremy Aldana

Though we hadn't known them that long, for any real comparisons, we had never seen Jimmy so happy before. Cindy tried to cover it up, but we could tell that she was excited too, even if she'd never admit to it.

# BOYS WILL BE BOYS

## Campouts
## Fall 1991

Before school started, we had one final campout in my backyard. We invited Jimmy and Cindy and told them it was the second best campout of the year. The best one was at the end of the year, on the night of our last day of school, to celebrate our upcoming freedom. We told them that this one was special though, and all they had to bring was their flashlights, their sleeping bags, and their signed contracts; the rest was up to us.

We always held the campouts at my house, cause I had the biggest backyard, which every year meant less and less. But, when we were younger, when Jake and Bobby used to camp out with us, we had a blast scaring the crap out of each other. In the backyard, mom used to have these huge lilac and rose bushes that were spread out all over the yard. The trees and bushes were so spread out that Brad once joked that he was sure that mom was hosting the 'annual gardener's obstacle course', where they had to run through the maze of bushes, trees, and plants, pruning and shearing along the way. It was silly, but it sure was funny then.

On a serious note though, those bushes along the high wooden fence with their six-inch breaks between the boards did wonders for the shadows. It was like they teamed up with the moon, just to scare us.

We'd start the nights out by watching movies like, 'Friday the 13th' and 'A Nightmare on Elm Street', you know, the really scary ones, to get us good and prepared for the night ahead. Then we'd go into the backyard, get in the tent, zip it up, and quickly turn on our flashlights (before we completely freaked ourselves out). What came next, after we all picked our places and settled inside, was a good round of scary stories. We'd pass around the big flashlight. Jake once told me that it was called, an 'Industrial Flashlight', whatever that was.

# BOYS WILL BE BOYS

When it was our turn, we'd make the others turn off theirs, and then we'd click on the big one. We'd hold it under our chin, against our chests, and tell our stories. We'd tell stories that we'd heard over the years, no doubt campfire stories passed on through the ages. Some were so scary that we could tell them 50 times and they'd still freak us out.

What you had to do, to get the perfect effect, while telling your story, was to lean your body slightly down and tuck your chin in 'ever-so-slightly'. It was a subtle move, but one that was necessary to get just the right freaky kind of shadow.

We all had our routines, if you could call them that, of how we told our stories. I always had to go first, for some reason. It was alright though, cause I'd lower my voice, talk slow, and turn the light out just a second before the end of the story. I'd wait another second or so, and then with one hand still on the flashlight, I'd use the other one to grab the arm of whoever was next to me at the exact moment I clicked my light back on and said the final words of the story.

I was sure to get at least one of the boys every time. I usually got socked in the arm or hit by some flying object, which was usually a 'Twinkie' or a 'Fruit Roll-Up'. When I was done with my story, I passed the light to whomever I grabbed. I'd always joke and tell the boys that I was just motivating them, to help get them into the zone.

Mark never seemed to be able to remember any scary stories he'd heard, so he'd just retell a scene from a scary movie. It was cool though, on account that he'd really get into it and recreate the scariest scenes to a 'T'. Jack would always tell us about some gruesome football injury that had happened in a game, or in a highlight that he saw. He was good, too, cause he'd put us right there on the fifty yard line and reenact the play for us.

It always ended with Jack making some kind of crackling noise that we took to be some poor guy's leg or

170

arm. Or, he'd tell us about some wide receiver getting drilled, while crossing the middle of the field. He'd have a bag of chips ready and just at the right moment, he'd click off the light for a second. We'd be right there, crossing the middle and just as we caught the ball, somehow Jack managed to 'pop' the bag of chips at the perfect moment, causing us all to drop the pass.

When we all groaned out loud, we'd look over at Jack, who'd be looking as sinister as Lawrence Taylor, the meanest and toughest 'SOB' to ever put on a Giants uniform. Then he'd open the rest of the bag, and just sit there and munch on the crumbs while we recovered from the hit.

Brad and Paul, probably cause they were so close, usually told their stories together. One would start the story and the other would finish it. They'd usually tell us hero type stories, far from scary, but they were always entertaining. They'd usually be about some bully getting their 'Come-Up-

Ins', in the end. You know; stories where the bullies ended up being bullied or laughed at.

Mom used to call it 'Karma', when bullies got what was due to them. She'd always tell Paul that he could gain some satisfaction in knowing that Karma was going to get those bullies in the end. She'd always refer to Karma as a 'she' and say, "Karma's gonna get them, if they're not careful" or if we did something that hurt someone else and then joked about it. She'd say, "She's gonna get you guys, if you don't cool it."

Dr. Ron said that mom made Karma a woman, on account that she probably had some tough times, herself, growing up and it was her way of coping. If he was right, then the Karma looking out for Paul was a 'he', and his name was Brad.

Andy was sure to tell us all a good scary story, every time. He'd always tell us ones about kids that were home alone. I think he told us those ones, cause he was usually the kid that was home alone the most, even though his folks were there. He'd tell the scariest one of all of us, on account that every kid has experienced that fear of being home alone, when some 'madman' was out in the neighborhood, and was trying to get into homes to hurt or kill kids.

See, us boys spent a lot of time at home alone, just like most kids our age did, on account that our folks usually had to work in order to pay all the bills. It never failed, we always hear stories about predators calling the house and asking the kids, who answered the phone, if their parents were home or not. The unfortunate kids that were never taught that lesson were the ones who said, "no," and then ten minutes later, they'd hear a knock at the front door. It was those kids who ended up with their picture on the sides of 'Milk Cartons'. That's why Andy's stories were the scariest, cause chances were he was just retelling stories he saw on the news or read in the paper.

# Jeremy Aldana

## The Scariest One
## Fall 1991

The scariest one Andy ever told was the one where a kid would be home at night, alone, and the phone would ring. The kid then hesitates in answering it, cause he'd heard the stories before and is being cautious. The kid then decides to answer it, cause it might be his friends or his folks calling, but soon gets a rude awakening. He then answers the phone, just as he had been taught to do.

"Hello?"

Right after the words left his lips, he got a little scared, cause he realized that it was too late for his friends to call and his folks' movie was still playing at the theater. Then a slight panic and fear came over him as he said "hello" again. But, this time, all he hears is heavy breathing. The kid then hangs up and desperately hopes that it was just a wrong number. Then he waits a few minutes by the phone to see if it was gonna ring again, not even thinking of what he's gonna do if it is some creep.

After ten minutes or so, the kid thinks and forces himself to believe that it's one of his buddies messing with him; playing a prank on him, cause it was always fun to scare the crap out of your friends for some reason. He's then convinced that it's one of his friends and tries to figure out which one of them was capable of pulling off this kind of prank. He goes down the list in his head, and tries to remember which ones he told that he'd have the house to himself that night.

Twenty minutes pass by and the kid thinks he knows for sure who is messing with him, and now he's thinking about all the different cruel and sadistic ways he was gonna get his buddy back, when the phone rings again. Of course, the kid jumps when the phone rings and then while it's ringing, he calls himself a 'wuss' for being scared. By the third ring, he's ready to let his friend know that he knows who it is, and just how bad they're gonna have to pay.

However, when the kid picks it up, he decides he'll play along with the prank for a minute and not say anything. In fact, the kid is so sure of himself that he plays along too well and starts breathing heavy into the phone. Then, after about thirty seconds of that, the kid decides to call out his bud (this is where Andy inserted our names to scare us even more).

"Joey, I know it's you and you're gonna pay big-time pal!"

But, when the breathing, on the other end of the phone gets heavier, and thus creepier, and doesn't respond to the call out, the kid repeats himself. He calls out his bud again.

"Joey, I know it's you, come on now, the jokes over!"

However, when the caller just keeps breathing heavier and heavier, not saying a word, the kid begins to list off all of

176

his friends, calling them out one by one, waiting for them to respond. He repeats his callout after each name on his list, getting tougher and thus more scared after each name.

"Come on, Paul, I know it's you, you jerk, now knock it off! Okay, Mark, joke's over, real funny, now quit it; you're starting to freak me out! Alright, Jack, you got me, now please stop! Okay, Brad, so one of the boys put you up to this, you can stop now! Okay, Paul, joke's over for real this time! Knock it off! Say something, you jerk! I'm really getting freaked out, here! Really, say something, you jerk! I won't be mad, just say something already!"

When only the breathing continues and no words are spoken, the kid freaks out and slams down the phone, wishing that his folks would get home soon. After slamming the phone down, he notices that his whole body is shaking and can't seem to think straight. He's more scared than he's ever been in his life, and the only thought he has, is that of wishing his parents would get home.

After a few minutes of silence, in his head and in the house, he realizes just how eerie the quiet is and runs around turning on every television set and radio, just to hear their sounds. Then, nothing happens for another ten minutes and the kids starts to turn down all the television sets and radios, and tries to think of who might be messing with him. He acknowledges the fact that it might be some bad guy, but then convinces himself that, stuff like that only happened in the movies or to other people, and wouldn't ever happen to him.

The kid then starts to regain his thoughts, and goes down the list in his mind again trying to remember if he messed with one of them and this is only payback owed to him. But, then, he realizes that he hasn't messed with anyone to deserve this kind of revenge and suddenly remembers that he hadn't told any of his friends that he was going to be alone that night. That's when the terror starts for the kid, as he knows that he's in trouble for real.

# BOYS WILL BE BOYS

The phone then rings again and, out of fear, the kid chooses not to answer it. He quickly comes to the conclusion that if he doesn't answer it, then the bad guy will think he left the house, and will then go away, on to someone else as long as it wasn't him anymore. After the phone rings ten times, the sound of the phone becomes eerie, just like the silence did after the last call.

As it keeps ringing, the kid can't remember the phone number to the police station, and can't remember where his folks kept the phone book. Then, at about the twentieth ring, he runs to the kitchen to check on the fridge, hoping that his folks left the number to the theater behind a magnet or on the counter, on a piece of paper with the emergency numbers. Then, the phone stops ringing and the kid lost track of how many rings it rang, as if it had anything to do with the creep who let it ring, like it somehow meant something important if it rang twenty-five times.

As he walked in circles, he remembered his folks had tried to give him the theater's and the police station's numbers, before they left, but he told them that he was old enough and didn't need them, that he wasn't a little kid anymore. Then, he starts to curse himself, calling himself 'stupid' and an 'idiot' and stuff, for his tough guy act earlier in the night. Then, he gets hopeful for a moment, as he realizes that the creep could've stopped calling and maybe that was actually his parents calling, and letting it ring all those times, figuring that since he had the house to himself, that he was probably in his room listening to his 'boom box' real loud.

Time then passed in 'slow-motion' for the kid, fear and worry clogging up his head, waiting for something to happen. He wished his parents would call, so he could tell them about the calls and beg them to come home right away. He'd tell them that he was sorry for acting tough earlier, if they came home right away. Then the phone rings again, and he picks it up on the first ring, and in a scared voice, he quickly says, "hello?"

He was half hoping and half expecting his parents to be on the other end of the line. He wouldn't care this time, he'd let his mom call home, cause she was worried and he wouldn't be mad at all. But, when no one says anything on the other end, and all he hears is the creepy heavy breathing again, he lashes out and gets mad.

"LISTEN, YOU SICK FREAK, YOU BETTER KNOCK IT OFF OR I'M CALLING THE COPS!"

Then, the kid slams down the phone, only to have it ring the next second. He then quickly thinks that if he acts 'super tough' instead of scared, he'll scare the creep away. When he grabs the phone on the second ring, he yells into it right away.

"LISTEN, YOU FREAK, QUIT CALLING ME!"

Then, the kid waits and expects to hear more heavy breathing, but instead hears his mother gasp and yell back into the phone.

"What did you just call me?"

The kid quickly explains himself and says sorry a bunch of times. His mother then gives the phone to his dad, who tells him that they are stopping on their way home, to get 'a bite to eat'. His heart skips a beat and he feels more alone than he ever has before. He then tells his dad about the calls, and begs him to come home and even offers to cook them food, as long as they get home right away.

Unfortunately, for the kid, his dad tells him that it must be one of his friends playing a prank on him and to not worry too much about it. His dad then told him that they'd be home in a while, so he had nothing to worry about. He then hangs up the phone and fights to keep himself from crying. He knows by now that it's some creep calling and not his friends messing with him, like his dad said. He had a feeling that his folks would tell him that, but still hoped,

somewhere in his heart, that they would believe him and rush

home to assure him and protect him.

The kid then realizes he's on his own and starts to run

around the house, looking for something that could be used

as a weapon to protect himself, but could only think of a

knife to use. After realizing that he wouldn't even know how

to use it, let alone use it to stab the creep if and when he

showed up. He then decides that if the creep does shows up,

he was gonna make a run for it, but was torn because he

didn't want to leave the house and have his folks come home

to the creep in the house. He decides to stay, then changes

his mind several more times, until the phone rings again.

The kid let it ring three times and picked it up, hoping

with all of his might that it's his folks calling to tell him they

had a change of heart and are on their way home. He makes a

mistake and assumes it's his folks, and as he picked up the

phone, he says, "So, are guys on your way home now?"

183

The kid stopped talking and waited to hear his mom or dad's voice on the other end, but didn't. And in the briefest of moments, he's relieved that he didn't hear any breathing. But, what the kid did hear made every single hair on the back of his neck and on his arms stand up. In the most terrifying and ominous tone of voice the kid ever heard, came the scariest sentence.

"I'm two blocks away."

The kid had never heard such a creepy voice, and the eerie calmness in which the creep spoke sent shivers throughout his whole body. The kid didn't have to hang up this time, cause the creep hung up first. No heavy breathing, just the creepy voice, and now the kid's really freaking out. He tries to remember where he put his knife but can't, and then tries to think of where all the best hiding spots in the house were, but didn't know, cause they just moved there a few months ago.

# BOYS WILL BE BOYS

When the phone rings again, the kid picks it up and listens, but doesn't talk right away. He hears that creepy, freaky voice tell him that he's only one block away now. Then in desperation, he yells out, "You don't know where I live!"

He almost has a heart attack when the creep tells him his exact address. The kid then slams down the phone and just stares at it, wishing that his folks were home, cause he knows that now he can't think straight. Out of fear and confusion, the kid answers the phone when it rings again seconds later.

"I'm two houses away."

The kid then takes the cordless phone with him, locks himself in his room, and answers it again on the first ring, when it rang seconds later.

"I'm in the house."

The kid is scared out of his mind now, grabs his flashlight, turns out his bedroom light, and runs into his closet. He knows only minutes had passed, even though they

185

felt like hours. He hears noises coming from downstairs and he's close to being scared to death. Then he hears footsteps coming up the stairs, and knows he's toast for sure.

It was at this point when Andy slowed his voice, way down, for effect and switched off his flashlight to finish the story.

The kid then hears the footsteps getting closer to his room, and then hears his bedroom door open and close. He then hears the steps getting louder, as they got closer to his hiding spot. He looks up to see the doorknob start to turn slowly, and knows he's a goner for sure. And, just as he's about to scream, (this is where Andy flips his light back on) the door flies open, only to have his dad looking down at him.

The kid's heart nearly leaps out of his chest, as he jumps up and hugs his dad while yelling at him, and crying. His folks told him that they were worried about him and decided to come home to make sure he was okay, instead of going out to eat. The kid's relieved at this point; shaken up a bit, but otherwise fine. He then falls asleep after a few hours, only to be woken up by the sound of the phone ringing downstairs.

The kid lets it ring a few times before leaving his room, and then walks downstairs. Then, just as the kid picks up the phone, he hears a knock at the door, and the fear from earlier in the night comes back. He hopes he's only dreaming, or maybe he was just sleepwalking. Then, the knocking stops, and then the ringing stops, and the kid decides to believe he dreamt the phone ringing and knocking at the door, and that he actually slept-walk down the stairs.

Feeling relieved that it was just his imagination; the kid decides to put the phone down and check out the front window, towards the front door, just in case. When he sees no one there, he calls himself a 'wuss', like before, and decides to check the outside for himself, again, just in case. Little did the kid know that the scariest thing he would ever see was waiting for him to turn around. The creep from the phone was inside the house, inches from the kid, just waiting for him to turn around.

The heavy breathing was what let the kid know he hadn't been dreaming or sleepwalking at all. And as the kid turned around, for what would be his last time ever making such movements, the heavy breathing stopped. In that very moment, possibly the kid's last, he saw where the breathing came from. The kid looked directly into the shallowest black eyes he ever had the displeasure of seeing, and the last thing the poor kid ever saw was the sinister smirk the creep had plastered on his face. And the last thing the kid ever heard was that eerily calm voice breathe into his ear, the words, "I never left the house."

None of us ever knew how or even why Andy had made up such a story, but it freaked us all out the first and only time we heard it. In preparation for Cindy and Jimmy's big night, we all made Andy promise not to tell that one.

Andy reluctantly agreed, and told us all that it was fine, on

account that he'd think of a better one, anyway.

# Jeremy Aldana

## Vicious Cycle
## Fall 1991

We had the campout on Friday night, in my backyard as usual, and we were all ready to make the night official. Cindy and Jimmy were going to be sworn in as members of 'The Boys', which was an honor bestowed on few. We joked, before they got there, that it was like we were 'knighting' them, like how the Queen of England knights people.

We had no doubt that they were gonna memorize the rules we gave them, as cheesy as it was. There were only a few to learn, and they were easy enough, on account that they were all implied. The first was that family came first, and the boys were family. The second was to always be there for each other, no matter what. And the third and final rule was that you never 'rat', and you never run away from your problems. It was never about the rules, but was about commitment to each other. It was about the trust we had in each other, and the loyalty that grew from it. We were a family, which meant that we were there for each other, forever, no questions asked.

As we were all like brothers, and since we were going to add another brother, Jimmy, and a sister, Cindy, into our group, it made Jack's idea even sweeter. He had the idea to scare them, as in an initiation, but we all thought better of it, until he came up with an even better one. His better idea wasn't to scare them at all, but to cement their commitment into the group right along with our renewed one. I don't remember where we ever heard the idea before, maybe in a movie or something, but we had all heard about it along the way. And what better way to show your allegiance to your brothers, than to become 'blood-brothers'.

We didn't want Cindy and Jimmy to know that we had never done the blood-brother ritual before, so we got to the tent early. Well, Brad and I set it up, so we were already there, but the rest of the boys came shortly after that. It was

Jeremy Aldana

about five o'clock when we zipped up the tent and settled in, ready to take our own initiation.

We made a plan before we started and made sure Mark brought his knife. We all propped our flashlights up around the tent, and then glued our eyes on Mark, as he pulled out his Rambo knife. None of us knew where Mark got the knife from, but it looked like something 'Rambo' would use. Brad always had a fear that Mark was gonna pick a fight one day with someone who he couldn't beat up, and he was gonna be worse off for it. Mark had already been kicked out of our Junior High for fighting, but we weren't as concerned that he was gonna end up in prison one day, as we were that he was gonna end up dead someday, as a result of a fight gone bad.

What was weird about Mark, though, was that he never picked a fight with someone, whom he felt didn't deserve it. Instead, he picked fights with those who pushed around weaker people, who couldn't defend themselves. I

192

guess you could say that he was noble, or stupid, or maybe

they went hand-in-hand. Either way, Mark was on a path of

eventual destruction, and none of us knew for sure that we

could change that.

Knife in hand, Mark asked us if we were ready and we

nodded 'yes', but Brad shot his hand up first to address the

group. He wanted to make sure that we had all the supplies

we needed; not just for us, but for Cindy and Jimmy too.

Andy spoke up after that, on account that he was in charge of

getting the supplies together. I think Andy's fears were

somewhat relieved when he got to take control of some part

of what we were all involved in.

Dr. Ron once told me that people, like Andy, who

craved approval and love, but rarely ever got it, had built fears

inside themselves. He said those fears allowed them to always

have an excuse to never put themselves in situations where

they could be disappointed, thus not hurt so much. He called

it a 'vicious cycle', whatever that meant. He explained it better when he told me that those same people, with that built-in fear, like Andy, were usually the most loyal and committed people we'd ever come across in our lives. He also told me that when those people take stake in something they believe in, despite their fears, they will find a way to do what's needed to complete their tasks.

In Andy's case, that was giving him a job to do. Jack, Paul, or Mark probably wouldn't ever really understand (I barely do), but Brad knew exactly what Dr. Ron was talking about. He always made sure that Andy had a job to do, and you know what, Andy never failed.

# BOYS WILL BE BOYS

## Supplies
## Fall 1991

Our supplies consisted of a gallon of water, a stack of band-aids, a couple of rolls of gauze, and a roll of medical tape. Andy got the nod from Brad, to pass out the band-aids, strips of gauze, and tape to each of us. We all had our own canteens full of water; the gallon was for refills, and for Cindy and Jimmy. When we all had our supplies in front of us, we all nodded to Brad, one-by-one, telling him that we were ready; that we understood there was no turning back.

We didn't want to cut ourselves a bunch of times and shake each other's hands one-by-one, as we were tough, but not stupid. Our plan was to pass Mark's knife around and each of us slice into our left palm, and cup our hands so we didn't bleed all over the tent. Then, when we were all done slicing our palms, we would shake each other's hands firmly. We didn't cut into our left palms cause we were right-handed (which we were, by the way), but because we would need our right palms to cut again when Cindy and Jimmy were sworn in.

Mark cut first, then Andy, then Paul, then Jack, then Brad, and then me. We all cut, and we all grimaced a bit, not because it hurt, but cause it felt weird to cut into our own flesh, even though we cut only far enough to get a small pool of blood in our hands. It actually stung for a second, and then our palms itched. It was actually kinda funny watching the boys fighting the urge to scratch their palms. It was like how when you get your haircut and the hair would fall on your nose, and you'd desperately want to itch it, but knew you couldn't, on account that you didn't want to tick off the person cutting your hair, cause you didn't want them messing up.

After a minute or so, I noticed the boys staring at me, on account that they saw me with a big grin on my face. "Oh, come on guys, you all look like you got ants in your pants!"

None of us were prepared for what Andy said next, though.

"Are we gonna do this or what? You guys aren't scared, are you?"

It was the first time we ever heard Andy callout anybody, let alone all of us at the same time. I guess ole' Jack was wearing off on him, after all.

We weren't about to let Andy show us up, so seconds after he issued his callout, we all starting shaking each other's hands. It took about thirty seconds for all of us to shake hands. Then, we all went quiet while we patched up our wounds. Sure it was just a small cut and a firm handshake, but the feeling I got from truly becoming blood-brothers with the boys, was one that I'll never forget. We were all connected now, our bonds of brotherhood cemented by our own blood! When I looked up, I knew in an instant that the boys felt the same, cause they were all smiling just as big as I was.

Mark put the knife back in his backpack after he cleaned it, and then we all started talking, at the same time, about what we just did. I heard everybody telling Jack what a great idea it was, and knew he loved all the attention. His face lit up, like he just got 'the last golden ticket' from a 'Wonka Bar'! Brad then suggested we all clean up the garbage and check out each other's tape jobs, so Cindy and Jimmy wouldn't notice too much before we told them.

# BOYS WILL BE BOYS

## The Quiz
## Fall 1991

Cindy and Jimmy showed up right at seven o'clock, as scheduled, with their gear. After we all scrunched in, it took about a second for Jimmy to notice our hands. I knew, on account that I watched Jimmy's eyes go around the tent, but he didn't say anything about them right away.

Brad took the lead, which I appreciated, when Cindy and Jimmy put their sleeping bags down, sat cross-legged, and switched on their flashlights. I was still watching Jimmy, on account that he went from watching me to each one of the boys. I think I noticed, because it wasn't the same way he usually looked at us. In a weird kinda way, it was like we were busted, but I think I was the only one to feel that way.

It was like he was looking at us in the disapproving way a teacher looks at you when she catches you passing a note. I kinda had the feeling that we had done something wrong, and I was itching to callout Jimmy on his glances. He hadn't said a word about what he was looking at though. For a moment, I thought maybe I was imagining it, cause Jimmy was just a kid like us. He was about to become one of the boys, and that meant there was no way he could be looking down on us.

However, as Brad was quizzing Cindy on the rules (which she recited perfectly back to him), I thought about how fitting it would be for Jimmy to actually be disappointed in us, only on account that we boys were brutally honest with each other. We boys usually didn't hold much back, and as Andy proved earlier, and Mark with Jack, and Jack with Jimmy when we first met him, it would fit perfectly that on Jimmy's initiation night, that he would call us out.

I was barely listening to Brad quiz Jimmy, when I noticed Cindy looking at me. What startled me, more than Jimmy's earlier disapproving glances, was that when I made eye contact with Cindy, I saw concern in her eyes. It was weird, cause she had been smiling only moments before when she recited her answers. With Jimmy's glances and Cindy's concerned eyes, I was as confused as 'a deer caught in headlights'.

I had heard the expression from my uncle, who told me that there were tons of deer in Wisconsin and when they jump out on the highway, in front of cars at night, instead of getting out of the way, sometimes they slow down or stop right in the middle of the road and just stare into the car's headlights. My uncle said that it was like they were hypnotized by the lights or something, and couldn't move. I didn't have to be a 'rocket scientist' to know how it ended for the deer. Anyway, if it's possible, I think I knew what those deer might have felt in their last moments.

What I couldn't figure out, was why they were acting so weird, and why I was the only one to notice. What was even more weird was that as soon as Jimmy was done, perfectly reciting the rules, he gave out a big ole' sigh and laugh that was echoed by each of the boys. When I looked back at Cindy, after turning to look at Jimmy, I noticed she was crying and smiling at the same time. Now, I knew that girls were complex and everything like that, but this one was new to me. Even after spending all that time with Cindy and learning about girls, smiling and crying at the same time was never covered. Don't get me wrong, we all had seen talk shows and movies where women would cry and smile, but none of us had ever seen it in real life before. We knew that mother's cried when they gave birth, cause they were happy and couldn't contain their emotions, and we knew that those women were adults who had lived a life full of experiences that would warrant such complex reactions to their emotions, but Cindy was just a girl, only a couple years older than me.

I didn't understand right away, but I learned a lot about Cindy in that moment that changed everything for me. She was crying cause she saw how happy Jimmy was, and again I didn't have to work for 'NASA' to know that for whatever reasons she had, seeing how happy her brother was at that moment was the most important thing in the world to her. That alone could've secured her a place with the boys.

After the laughing calmed down and the pats on Jimmy's back were complete, I noticed that the silence that followed came with everyone's eyes on me. As usual, I became the spokesperson for the boys, and I was okay with that. However, I had to take a second to figure out my next move, on account that I saw how Jimmy and Cindy had looked at me at different times, since they got there.

"Go ahead, Joey!"

Jack had no problem breaking the silence to holler at me, even though he was only a few feet away.

"Hold on, Jack!"

And of course, I had no problem hollering back at him. I knew the boys hadn't noticed the way Jimmy had looked at them, and the way that Cindy had looked at me. I knew that our plan wasn't going to go the way we had intended it to.

"Guys, they know already." The boys then had that 'deer in the headlights' look on their faces. "Yea, guys, they both know already. I saw them notice when they came in, and I don't think they approve."

The tent full of deer were silent, until Jimmy spoke up.

## Wake Up Call
## Fall 1991

Jimmy had our attention, just like he usually did when he spoke up.

"Listen you guys, there's something I need to tell you. Remember, in the park, when I told you about my accident?"

I saw the boys nod right along with me, but didn't hear a peep from them.

We talked about it for days, after he told us about how he got his limp. It had been what Dr. Ron would've called a 'wake up call', where we were all supposed to learn some kind of life lesson that would serve to make us better people. Jimmy's story was certainly eye opening and made us really think. There was no doubt that not only would we all remember what he told us that day, for the rest of our lives, but there was a good chance that we were gonna pass on the lesson to our kids one day in the future.

205

We'd all heard about accidents happening to kids, like the one Jimmy had, but never knew anyone that it happened to. What Jimmy did, wasn't the brightest move a kid could make, even he admitted as much. None of us called him stupid or anything, on account that we've all made our fair share of mistakes, and just like Jimmy had his limp, we all had scars and stories and punishments that we had to deal with. Heck, even though Jack did the right thing in beating his dad senseless and sending him to prison, Jack still spent time in Juvenile Hall.

Jimmy told us that what happened was his fault, but what was weird was that he was so detached from it. When he told us what happened, he didn't cry and he didn't brag about it. Not crying or bragging about a scar or something crazy or scary that happened to you, was like not getting excited when you caught a foul ball at County Stadium. We didn't really understand why he was the way he was about it, but we talked and figured it was just his way of living with it, and we could live with that.

That morning, in the park, he told us about how he and his friends made the mistake no kid ever wanted to make. He told us that his parents went out to dinner and left Cindy in charge. He said that him and his friends kept bugging Cindy to go out to the mall with her friends, until she couldn't take all the whining anymore. He promised her that they'd be alright, and that they wouldn't tell their folks. After she left, he told us that him and his friends ran upstairs to their parent's room.

Jimmy told us that his dad was a cop and kept his duty gun in a shoebox on the top shelf of his closet, underneath a pile of folded sweaters. He told us that his dad had told him and Cindy that his gun was off-limits to them. You know, stuff about fingers being broken and groundings for life.

207

# Jeremy Aldana

He told us that after they got the gun down; they passed it around and pointed it at each other like they were cops themselves, stopping the bad guys. He said that he was smart enough to know that pointing a loaded weapon at each other wasn't the best idea, and had seen enough movies to know that he should empty the gun first. He said that he took the gun back and pulled out the clip, which he told us was also called a magazine. He told us that he took each bullet out and put the empty clip back in the gun. He then said that one of his friends told him that there still might be one bullet left in the chamber. And just to prove his friend wrong, that the gun was empty, he squeezed the trigger.

When he told us in the park, he showed us how he had held the gun at his side just in case his friend was right, so he didn't shoot himself. And of course, judging by his limp, we knew his friend had been right. He told us that he'd never fired a gun before then, and hasn't since. He said that when it went off, it kinda jolted his body, like someone shook him by his shoulders. He said the jolt must've made his hand jerk towards his body, cause he ended up shooting himself in the leg; his thigh actually.

Now, we were no doctors or anything, so when he told us that there was a 'main artery', whatever that was, in his leg, we took his word for it. He told us that he went into some kind of shock. He said his friends freaked out, and all he could hear was the loudest ringing in his ears he'd ever heard. He said that he hit the ground and dropped the gun but never cried, to which we were all impressed in a stupid kinda guy way.

He said that after the ringing stopped, one of his friends raced downstairs and called '911'. He said the lady on the 911 call told his friends to get a belt and tighten it around his thigh, to stop all the bleeding. He said that he felt stupid, but also brave in a weird way, cause he stayed as alert as he could and was able to tell his friends the restaurant his folks went to.

# Jeremy Aldana

Jimmy didn't remember how much blood he lost or how long it took the ambulance to get there, but remembered the pool of blood he was sitting in and the slurping suction noise that was made when the paramedics pulled him off the ground. The police showed up with the ambulance and started drilling him and his friends, as the ambulance guys tried to fix him up enough to take him to the hospital. He said he told them that it was all his fault, and that his dad was a cop too. He said that they took him to the emergency room, and told him that he had to have surgery, on account that the bullet hit the main artery inside his leg.

He told us that his folks were at the hospital, when he came out of surgery, but Cindy still hadn't shown up. She hadn't gotten back from the mall until late that night, and a cop was waiting to take her to the hospital. He said his folks were disappointed in him, but that they were just glad that he was alive. Cindy, on the other hand, he told us, felt real bad for leaving him alone, and got in major trouble from their folks.

He told us, that morning in the park that he knew she still blamed herself; even though he told her about a hundred times that it was his fault alone. I guess we kinda could understand how they both felt.

# Jeremy Aldana

## Subconscious Thingy
## Fall 1991

Jimmy still had our attention, just like he did in the park when he first told us about his accident. This time, though, while he retold us the short version, I felt Cindy grab a hold of my hand and move close to me. I didn't understand it, but I turned and looked at her wet eyes, instinctively pulled her closer, and allowed her to hug me.

Cindy hugged me tight and began to cry harder, pulling the boys' attention from Jimmy to her. I looked at them, noticed their confused faces, and waved them off with my left hand, as Jimmy starting talking again. I could feel her warm tears on my chest and I just hugged her back, letting myself be there for her. I hadn't cried like that before, even after what happened to mom, Jake, and Bobby, but I wanted too.

Jimmy continued, after glancing my way, and I got the feeling that he wanted to make sure that I was there for his sister in that moment. I didn't know what to think of it; that Jimmy was now giving me his approval where earlier he showed me the opposite. It was like he was trying to not only protect his big sister, but us as well. I guess, after going through what he had been through, you could say that he was 'wise beyond his years'. That's what adults say about extraordinary kids who show class and poise years before the world thought they should.

Next to my mom and brothers, I never felt closer to anyone as I did to the boys. However, when I hugged Cindy back, I understood a new kind of closeness, and I'm still not a hundred percent sure what that means. I didn't feel, at all, like I was betraying either, on account that the closeness was different this time. It wasn't a crush feeling or anything like that, but was a deeper connection. I think we needed each other, as weird and dramatic as it sounds, cause we both had huge crosses to bear.

# Jeremy Aldana

I heard Dr. Ron talk about me having 'a cross to bear', when it came to me accepting what happened to mom, Jake, and Bobby. He said that in order for me to grieve, heal, and move on, I had a cross to bear. He said that for some reason, I had this subconscious need to carry a burden around for what happened to my family. He said that my subconscious was my mind behind my brain. He told me to think of it like my sleeping mind, and said that's why we don't always remember our dreams. To that, I told him that I must've had a strong subconscious thingy, cause I always remembered my dreams.

Dr. Ron knew that I believed in Jesus and told me that to better understand what a cross to bear meant, that I needed only to think about how Jesus had died. He said that Jesus carried all of humanities burdens, when he literally carried the cross for us, to his death. He said that we were supposed to learn from that somehow, in our own ways. He told me, that if I truly believed in forgiveness from God, then

214

I should understand that Jesus was meant to bear our crosses and to carry our burdens for us, so we could go on living. He suggested that I think about that more; which I did.

Cindy felt responsible for Jimmy's accident, and I felt responsible for my family's accident, on account that they were driving to pick me up at Jack's house when they died. Maybe the reason we both held on to each other so tight, was because we were bearing each other's crosses.

## Transfix
## Fall 1991

I listened to Jimmy tell the boys about what happened after the accident, as I held onto Cindy.

"Guys, I never told you everything about my accident. I knew I was gonna have to tell you sooner or later, but I didn't know when the time would be right."

Even as I held onto Cindy, I was amazed to hear this little kid talk like he was a grown-up. I knew I needed to be there for his sister in that moment, but I knew I needed to hear what he had to say too.

"I hadn't planned on telling you guys, tonight. In fact, part of me wished I'd never have to tell you, but I can see your hands and know what you did. I may be a kid, but I'm not stupid."

When Jimmy said that, I got a flash from when I said those same words to the cops after Jack beat his dad with his Louisville Slugger. And no matter what Jimmy was gonna tell us, in those next few moments, I knew he was definitely one of us. When I sneaked a peek at the boys, after Jimmy said that, I saw their faces and knew they felt the same way.

"After my accident, the doctors in the ER told my folks that I needed a blood transfusion in order to survive. My folks agreed to it, and I got one just in time."

Jimmy had managed to talk in such a calm way, just like he did in the park that morning, that Cindy had slowed her crying, and began to relax a little. Even the boys lost the blank look on their faces. I know, cause I heard them all, in unison, ask, "What the heck is a blood transfusion?"

Dr. Ron told me that sometimes when people get real sick, like if they have a disease or something that a way they deal with it is to learn everything they could about it. He told me that it gives them a sense of having more control over their bodies, and their lives. He said that when viruses and diseases take hold of someone's body, the person feels like they have no more control. And he said that when people feel like they have no more control over themselves, they experience the worst feelings of their lives. By the way Jimmy articulated what a blood transfusion was to us, I kinda knew something worse was gonna follow.

I think Cindy was kinda impressed with how Jimmy explained it to us, cause she stopped crying altogether. She stopped hugging me and pulled back a little, sniffling quietly and wiping her tears. She didn't move away though, instead she pulled my right arm around her shoulder and leaned her head against my chest, as she watched her brother tell us about what happened. At that point, I got the feeling that Cindy already knew what Jimmy was gonna tell us, and I wondered if it would really get worse from there. It did, and to my surprise Jimmy stopped at times and let the boys ask questions, to which he answered as if he was 'Doogie Howser M.D'., himself.

Jimmy told us that a blood transfusion was when they gave a patient someone else's donated blood. They inject the new blood directly into the patient, so that the patient's heart didn't have to work extra hard trying to pump blood that the patient no longer had. He said that he got his because he had lost so much blood from the gunshot wound. Now, of course, he didn't explain it the way I did, but I didn't understand all the medical 'mumbo-jumbo' he used.

"Have you guys ever heard of HIV, or Human Immunodeficiency Virus?"

None of us had ever heard of HIV before that moment and I'm sure Jimmy could tell as much, on account of the solid round 'what's that', that filled the tent.

"Does it have to do with that blood transfix thing you had?"

The rest of the boys were now quiet, except Jack, who asked the question. We all knew that Jack took a special liking to Jimmy, since that first day and the monster shot he gave up to him. I guess it was out of respect for Jimmy, that none of us gave Jack any grief for his question. We all heard Jimmy clearly say 'transfusion', not transfix, so I'm sure Jack

could've got it right when he asked. I wondered, on account

that Jack was a lot smarter than he looked, if he was only

acting dumb to give Jimmy a chance to show his smarts.

Jack was like that, you know, if he feels that you

deserve the spotlight than he's gonna make sure you get it.

Dr. Ron said that Jack probably liked 'working behind the

scenes', cause he was such a big kid, and was always noticed

first and usually a part of most spotlights he was around. He

said that Jack probably enjoyed helping the most, when the

person he was helping didn't know it came from him. He said

that kids like Jack, with everything they went through,

sometimes grew up to be philanthropists, whatever they were.

I was so involved with Jimmy's story and Jack's

question, that I hadn't noticed Cindy sit up, until I heard her

say something to Jimmy.

"Ask them if they ever heard of AIDS, Jimmy."

# BOYS WILL BE BOYS

I kinda got the feeling, from the way she addressed Jimmy that she wanted him to get it over with, whatever 'it' was. I don't think any of us really knew what HIV was, but we all had heard of AIDS before. We didn't know much about it, and we certainly didn't talk about it in great detail or anything. I wondered what her and Jimmy were getting at, and wondered if any of the boys knew. My wonderment lasted only seconds, on account that Cindy pulled my arm back around her and leaned her head back on my chest.

I heard Jimmy ask us boys if we ever heard of AIDS, and listened as a mixed response of 'yea', 'sorta', 'no', and 'I don't knows'. Jimmy told us that it stood for Acquired Immune Deficiency Syndrome, and that only people with HIV get AIDS. He told us all the technical stuff he learned about HIV and AIDS, but I think we only understood some of it.

When Cindy started to cry again, I kinda knew what Jimmy was gonna say next.

"Guys, sometimes blood transfixes turn out to be not such good things. Sometimes the needles aren't clean, and sometimes the blood is bad. Bad blood means that it didn't get tested right, and the blood has a virus in it. Guys, I got some bad blood from the transfix."

I think that by Jimmy saying transfix instead of transfusion, he was trying to soften the blow he just delivered. And even though I kinda figured it out, I was still in shock that Jimmy had just told us that he had gotten the HIV.

# BOYS WILL BE BOYS

## Bad Blood
## Fall 1991

Jimmy was smart enough to know that we grew to care about him. Heck, we were all there that night to invite him and his sister into our family. I think he knew that we'd be in some kind of shock, and by using Jack's transfix; he was hoping to make it easier on us.

"Does that mean you're sick, Jimmy?"

Andy was the first to ask this time. Paul quickly followed with a question of his own, before Jimmy could answer Andy's.

"Is there a cure?"

Cindy was crying harder now, more than she was before, and I took that to mean that there wasn't a cure yet. Unfortunately, I had guessed right, cause Jimmy answered both Andy and Paul's questions within a single breath.

"Yea, Andy, I got some bad blood inside me and so yea, I guess you could say that I'm sick. And, no Paul, there isn't a cure for the HIV."

Jimmy went on to tell us that he got the HIV from the blood transfusion, but that he didn't have AIDS. I think he could tell we were still pretty confused, cause he explained what each meant. He told us that the HIV was like having a super-bad flu virus that slowly kills all the cells in your body. Of course, he explained it better than I did, but I was doing my best to understand it all and still be there for Cindy. He told us that the HIV could stay inside your body, killing your good cells from anywhere from one day to 15 years or even longer. He said that the HIV isn't deadly until it finally breaks down your body, and you get AIDS.

Jimmy explained, as we all watched him talk with his hands, like he tended to do, what AIDS was. As he was telling us that the AIDS stood for a weakened immune system disease, I saw each of the boys rubbing their palms with their free hands. I wasn't sure if they were rubbing their palms because their cuts hurt, or because they were thinking about their own blood. I also wasn't sure if they were just gonna let Jimmy keep talking, or if they were gonna pepper him with more questions. I sure wasn't ready for the boys to start asking each other questions. I heard Mark ask Brad what an immune system was, and looked up to see Jimmy turn towards Brad, as if to wait for Brad's answer.

"It's our cells and organs and tissues, working together to fight off the bad stuff that enters our bodies."

We all saw that Mark was still confused by Brad's answer, so Jack took over and explained it better.

"Mark, you know how when you get a cold and your body gets all tired and stuff?"

"Yea?"

"Well, that's your immune system getting beat up. Then you take some medicine, drink '7-UP', and get some sleep. The medicine has stuff in it that helps your immune system. You drink lots of 7-UP and sleep, so your body can fight off the cold. I think Jimmy's saying that the bad blood he got from the transfusion had the HIV stuff in it. I think he's trying to tell us that the HIV is like having a cold or flu that won't go away, no matter how much medicine you take or how much rest you get."

I think Jack explained it pretty good, at least to Mark's satisfaction anyway. Cindy stopped crying before Jack finished, but as much as I felt for Jimmy and what he must've been going through, I couldn't help feeling horrible for Cindy. The boys went silent again for what felt like hours, but really was only seconds, until Jimmy took back over.

"Listen guys, I'm not mad that you all did the blood-brother thing. In fact, I think it's cool that you wanted to make me your blood-brother. And you know what, if I didn't have the HIV, I would've done it right along with you."

# BOYS WILL BE BOYS

"So, that's why you gave us that look when you first came in?" I asked, as Cindy pulled herself back up from my chest.

"Yea, cause at first, when I saw your hands all taped up, I knew that you wanted me and Cindy to do it too. And that's when I knew that I had to tell you about my disease. Part of me wanted to tell you guys right away, when we first started hanging out, but another part of me wasn't sure how you'd react and so I never told you."

I looked around, in the dim light, and noticed the boys had all stopped rubbing their hands and were all just staring at Jimmy. I could easily see the deer look again, and wondered what it was going to take to snap them out of it. I knew the batteries were good in all of our flashlights, on account that we checked them earlier, but the light seemed dimmer.

Jimmy managed to snap the boys out of their daze, when he spoke next.

"So, how'd it feel guys?"

None of the boys answered at first, which I could understand, cause I was still a little bit caught off guard, myself.

"So, guys, how'd it feel?" This time I saw that he had a weird grin on his face when he asked.

"It was cool, Jimmy!"

"Paul!" The rest of us yelled at him, at the same time.

"No, it's okay, guys. I wanted to know how it felt, honest I did. It's okay, Paul, thanks for being honest."

I don't think Jimmy liked the silence as much as we didn't, cause he changed subjects and kept on going.

"So, did me and my 'big sis' pass? I mean, we recited the rules perfectly. So, do we get in? Are we now officially part of 'The Boys'?"

I knew what had to be done next, and so I spoke up as I squeezed Cindy's hand.

"Of course, you guys are in. You always were. We love you guys."

"Easy there, Joey."

And so it started, one-by-one. The boys pitched me a fine ration of crap for the next few minutes.

"Yea, Joey, easy there man, we're just kids."

"Yea, Joey, you ain't gotta get all mushy."

"Geez, Joey, we had no idea."

"Hey Joey, maybe Cindy could take you shoe shopping tomorrow."

I'm sure they didn't need any flashlights to see how red my face got in those few moments, as the boys were putting quite a beating on me. I was so embarrassed that I didn't even know who said what to me, so there was no chance of a good comeback. At least we were all laughing again, even Cindy, and so I guess it was worth it. All I could come up with was weak, to say the least.

"You guys are cold-hearted!"

And then it came fast and loud, and from all of them.

"Aww, we love you too Joey!"

I managed to mutter, "Et tu, Cindy?" before the boys, now including her and Jimmy, tackled me backwards on my butt.

# BOYS WILL BE BOYS

## Perceptions
## Fall 1992

Over the last year, we all grew a little bit closer to each other. We also had a special birthday campout for each of our birthdays, and like always, they were at my house. The one coming up was gonna be special though, on account that Cindy's golden birthday was only weeks away; she'd be 17 years old on September 17th.

A lot had changed for us in a year. It's weird, you know, how time always seems to move fast when we're enjoying something, and then seemed to move slowly when we weren't having any fun. Dr. Ron told me that our perception is the cause of that. He said that the 'actual' time never changed, as in it never slowed down or sped up, even if you moved the hands of a clock yourself. He said that when we're having fun, our perceptions weren't geared towards paying any attention to the time. When we weren't having any fun, our perceptions were geared towards watching a clock and thinking about the time, thus dwelling on it and making it seem that it was moving slower than it was.

I didn't really understand most of it until he told me to think of it like the old saying, 'a watched pot never boils', to which, at first, I became more confused. He told me that when a person sets a pot of water on a stove, to boil it (for cooking), they can't leave it alone. He said that they stir it and stir it, and can't leave it alone. He said that when they keep stirring it, the water never boils, it just simmers, and said that when we sit and dwell on something (time), it will never move as fast as we want it too, thus the water won't boil as fast as we want it to. He said that if we just sit back and let the heat boil the water on its own, then it will boil as fast as it can.

When he saw that I was still a bit confused, he tried another old saying. He said it's like paddling upstream, against the current, saying that no matter how much energy we exert; because we are going against the natural flow of the water that we were never going to get anywhere. I think he took the opportunity to teach me about my habit of worrying about stuff too much, as in it was never gonna to get me anywhere. That's what I took away from it, anyway. In a way, I guess that makes sense and it does fit within the whole perception thing.

Anyway, with all that said, the last year seemed to fly by for all of us. We were growing up, and we were still having as much fun as the world let us. Cindy and I were now 'going out', or as they'd say in the fifty's, 'going steady'. We usually saw each other every day, and she practically lived at my house. My aunt and uncle were cool with it, and her parents didn't seem to mind that much. I think they didn't mind as much, on account that on most nights she slept over, Jimmy did too.

Jimmy was self sufficient enough, cause he always brought his medicine and took it when he was supposed to. Cindy pretty much taught me how to look out for him, like she did. I'm not sure exactly why she taught me, but I think it's cause she trusted me and it also lifted her burden a little bit. She told me that Jimmy didn't really like it all that much, that she always watched to make sure he was okay, but said that he seemed to adjust to it and didn't give her too much grief about it. 'Brotherly Love' or something like that, I suppose.

We all got to meet their parents, and figured out pretty quick why they always tried to keep us away from them. They were all 'lovey-dovey' and stuff, which I guess was their right, but they seemed to try too hard. Dr. Ron said that they were 'overcompensating', because they felt so bad for Jimmy. He said that overcompensating meant that they tried too hard at one thing, so they could make up for another. Like how a parent might be a workaholic and overcompensate for being gone all the time, by spoiling their kids. Anyway, regardless of Jimmy's parents' 'overcompensating', none of us could imagine what it must be like to be them, to have to deal with their kid having to go

through with what Jimmy had to. Cindy wasn't bothered by

the extra attention they gave Jimmy, for two reasons (I think).

First, she gave him tons of attention, herself; only hers was in

another way, the role of the 'overprotective sister'. And

second, she still felt guilty for leaving him that day.

# Jeremy Aldana

## Camp Randall
## Fall 1992

Cindy was now a junior and the rest of us were all sophomores this year. We didn't make it official (us going out) until this past summer, but that was cool with me. I think maybe it's cause I wasn't a freshman anymore. Just like the whole corporate world out there, we had politics at school too. There was this order of things at school, like a ranking social system for teens.

High School wasn't so bad, not as scary as we all thought it would be, anyway. It sure was a lot bigger than middle school though. It had three floors and an elevator for kids who had wheel chairs, and who used crutches. Jimmy even had a key to it, but if you knew him, you weren't surprised at all that he never used it. Their parents (Jimmy and Cindy's), had a meeting with the principal, and then with the school board. They had meetings about Jimmy and about his having the HIV. He never went to any of the meetings, and that was cool with us. He told us that he didn't want any part of it, on account that back in Philly, he didn't have the best experience when he went to them.

Our school was pretty cool about having Jimmy go there. Most everyone was cool about it and most kids were nice enough to him. The principal was actually excited about Jimmy being at our school, which was a little weird, to say the least. All through grade school and middle school, the goal was to never meet the principal; on account that it meant that you were probably in some kind of trouble. So, you can see why it was a bit confusing to have so much interaction with the principal, and not be in trouble.

Nobody messed with Jimmy his whole freshman year; not one single bully, which was a bit weird. We all thought, for sure, that some dumb kid was gonna want to pick on him, cause he had a disease. Jimmy knew why nobody did though, and we pretty much agreed with him. He told us that nobody messed with him because Jack was always around. You have to admit that he was probably right, seeing as how Jack was, by far, the biggest and toughest kid in school (even as a freshman). He hadn't stopped growing his whole freshman year, and was now over six feet tall, and weighed around 250 pounds. Of course, he played football and wrestled too, where he made the varsity team on each.

He led our team in tackles and in rushing touchdowns. In high school, we play what 'they' call 'Iron Man Football', where players often times played both offense and defense. Coach had Jack listed as a running back and a middle linebacker, and I guess that was a good fit for Jack, cause he won a bunch of awards and honors. He led us to the conference title, and then to the State Championship Game, which we won. It was close, though, and we needed overtime to win. He rushed for three touchdowns, had ten tackles, one sack, one interception, and one of this touchdowns was the game winning one.

# BOYS WILL BE BOYS

He scored off a broken play to win the game. It was supposed to be a draw, but the quarterback fumbled the handoff and when Jack picked it up, he was almost nailed. Time was running out and we all held our breaths, waiting for the big hit, cause the other team had a linebacker that was just about as big as Jack was. The other team's Jack was chasing our Jack, like he had stolen something from him. Somehow, Jack got away and, believe it or not, managed to break like six tackles on his way to the end zone. The crowd went nuts, and our section led the way. We had never been to 'State' before, so pretty much half the city (it seemed) was there. We played at Camp Randall Stadium in Madison, where the Badgers played.

We were all proud of Jack for how good he did, but none of us was more proud than Jimmy was. Ever since that monster shot, he hit off Jack, they were like best friends. Sometimes, when we were all hanging out at my house playing Nintendo, they'd talk for hours. We never heard Jack talk that much in his whole life. To Jimmy's credit, though, the kid knew how to listen. Sometimes, I thought to myself, that Jimmy listened better than Dr. Ron did. I even thought that if Jimmy made it to be an adult, then he'd make a good psychiatrist. See, that was the thing about him; he always made you think. We didn't sit and just think about him all the time, especially when we all hung out. It was when we were away from him, thinking about life, that we'd think about him and his disease. We'd think about life and death, and all the thoughts and choices we made. Sorry, adults, but kids are capable of deep thought.

Jimmy told Jack about why he didn't like all the school meetings and stuff, and Jack told him that he should tell all of us and not just him, cause we deserved to know too. After Jack told him that, Jimmy then told us. Cindy started to cry once, but then Jimmy gave her a 'look', and as weird as it was, she stopped instantly. He didn't get mad at her for crying or anything, he just said that he got tired of everyone

240

crying because of him. He told us that his folks cried a lot, even though they tried to hide it most of the time. He said that it was depressing, and of course we understood.

# Jeremy Aldana

## Hand-Me-Downs
## Fall 1992

Jimmy told us about his last school, back in Philly, and how they weren't as understanding about his disease as our school was, nor were the kids as cool as we were. He told us that he cried more in one year than most people cried in their lifetimes, and that he vowed never to cry again. His 'never crying again' vow made sense to us, when we thought about why we'd never seen him cry. He told us that he would've rather have been beaten up a hundred times, than to be 'ostracized' the way he was at his old school.

None of us knew what that word meant, exactly, but we pretty much got the gist of it. I'm pretty sure it meant that the kids made him an 'outcast' and that meant that nobody wanted him around. We all knew how bad that must've sucked, but none of us knew like Andy did, and I guess that's why they got along so well. Andy had been ostracized by his own parents and Jimmy at his last school, and we felt terrible for them. It wasn't pity that we felt for them, on account that we boys didn't do pity. Instead, we all came together and made sure that each and every one of us mattered. Like how Andy always showed us his report cards and essays, and how Cindy became like Brad's sister after Mary skipped out on him and his family. Like how we went to every one of Jack's football games and wrestling meets and how we always made sure that we all pitched in and got Paul a new outfit every few months, so he wouldn't have to wear the torn up 'hand-me-downs' from his brothers.

Hand-me-downs weren't the world's worst things, on account that we understood that money didn't grow on trees at Paul's house and how it must've been hard to support all the kids in his family. However, hand-me-downs that have been handed down three and four times wasn't cool at all. When clothes got worn that much, they ripped and tore and had all kinds of permanent stains on them, which didn't make wearing them to high school an easy thing to do. Kids in high school could be brutal, and all of Paul's brothers took mega-rations of crap at school for always having the same clothes. We didn't want Paul to have to go through that, at all.

We didn't leave anyone out either. For Mark, we got him a used punching bag and hung it in my basement, on account that we knew he couldn't afford to get kicked out of high school, like he did in Junior High. And since we got that bag, he hasn't been in one single fist fight. For Cindy, well I took the lead in that area, but the boys did what they could. They all still asked her questions about girls and stuff, but they all brought around their prospective girlfriends to meet her. If Cindy didn't approve of them, then the boys didn't go out with them, simple as that. And I always made sure that she was treated like a queen, no matter what! I'd write the occasional poem for her, bring her roses, and always gave her compliments when she needed them.

Mom taught me years ago, that it was our duty as boys and later as men to appreciate girls and women. She said that everyone loves to get compliments and girls were no different, and she was right too. She told me that if they wore a nice outfit, then we should tell them that they looked nice. And if they fixed their hair up nice, then we should tell them that their hair looked nice. She always said that there was nothing 'finer', in the whole world, than a woman smiling. She also told me that if I didn't have anything nice to say, then I shouldn't say anything at all. However, in the same breath, she also said that if a woman was having a 'bad hair day' or thought she looked fat, and asked us what we thought, then we should still tell them that they looked nice. See, this is another reason why girls are so confusing, cause we're supposed to compliment them when they look their best, and also when they didn't. I asked Cindy about that once, and she agreed with mom, saying that girls are only asking us, in the first place, on account that they care about what we think. We had a responsibility not to let them down, when they cared enough to ask us, which makes sense I guess.

Last, but not least, the boys made sure that I mattered. For one, none of them ever asked to see my 'journal'. They all knew about it, for sure, saw me writing in it, but never once bothered me about it. Sometimes, though, I thought about showing it to them, but then decided that it was best if I kept it to myself.

Cindy always told me how 'sweet' she thought I was, and I still hear that darn choir sing, when she says that. She makes me feel that I'm important, and always listens when she thinks I need to vent. Another thing they all do for me is listen when I have a memory to share about mom, Jake, or Bobby. They listen and laugh at all the right times, never asking me to stop remembering. I think that's what matters most to me, being allowed to remember them.

# BOYS WILL BE BOYS

## Jimmy's List
## Fall 1992

There was one time, this past year, that wasn't the best experience for us. It was when Jimmy fell down the stairs at school. Jack had been walking ahead of him, just having left homeroom (they had homeroom together), when he heard Jimmy call his name; calm as could be, Jack told us. Jack turned right around, but couldn't catch Jimmy in time. Now, Jimmy didn't fall down a whole flight of stairs or anything, just five or six steps, but that was enough to break his leg. He made it down to the last step fine, banged up, he said, but okay otherwise. However, his leg got caught underneath him, and when he showed us later, we all grimaced as we imagined what it must've looked like. Not Jack though, he saw it, and didn't react like we did.

I think Jack didn't react like us, on account that he was there and told us that he didn't have time to make stupid faces. He was a big kid, so he didn't have a problem carrying

247

Jimmy to the nurse's office. He said that Jimmy didn't cry either, which of course came as no shock to us. He said that when he came flying back down the steps, he jumped over Jimmy, saw his leg underneath him, and simply carried him to the office. He said he didn't know how bad it was, but that Jimmy knew instantly and told him on the way to the office that he'd broken his leg. After the trip to the hospital, Jimmy had a cast, a blue one (his favorite color), and let us all sign it first, before the rest of the school got to. They all signed it, to the point where you couldn't see anything but signatures and funny little pictures.

The broken leg isn't what scared all of us, though, cause kids broke their legs and arms all the time. We had all signed plenty of casts in our lifetimes, but what scared us was that, with the HIV, broken legs were not always just broken legs, but sometimes worse. When a bone breaks, the bone is fused (which is like glued) back together, or at least in place, and then put into a cast so it can't move around and has time to heal. However, with Jimmy breaking his leg, it meant more than just putting it back together again.

First, the leg he broke was the same leg he'd accidently shot, which started this whole HIV thing he has to deal with. Second, when a person has the HIV, it makes their body weaker. It doesn't make their bone weaker necessarily, but it weakens the body itself, as in its cells and stuff. See, inside our bodies, we have these blood cells that are called white blood cells, though I'm guessing they just call them white, cause I don't think they're really white at all. Anyway, these white blood cells, called 'CD4 cells', are the cells that our body uses to fight off infections and the other stuff that make our bodies weak. When the HIV is in someone's body, it attacks these cells and they go way down in number, so your body doesn't have much of a defense against the virus. Keep in mind; the boys and I only knew what we did about Jimmy's disease, on account that he told us and asked us to pay attention.

When someone with the HIV gets a cold, it seems like the flu to them, where it's just a cold to us. And when they get the flu, it seems like phenomena to them. When people with the HIV die, it's not from the HIV itself, but from the AIDS. People can live a while with the HIV, before they get the AIDS, but because the disease is so new to people, the doctors don't know how long it takes to go from the HIV to the AIDS. Basically, if a person has the AIDS, then they had the HIV before that. Jimmy has the HIV, and the doctors tell him that one day he will get the AIDS. He says that, surprisingly enough, he hasn't met one doctor who felt pity for him, and he should know, too, on account of his pity radar.

Now, when Jimmy broke his leg, we all knew it was bad news, cause breaking a bone in your body throws your whole system out of whack. Your body has to heal itself, like with any ailment, and bones are no different. So, when Jimmy broke his leg, despite the cool blue cast he had on the outside, we knew his insides would suffer more. They did, and he got 'sicker than a dog' for the first two weeks and went to the doctor at least every other day.

The doctors told Jimmy and his folks that his white blood cell count was pretty low, and said he got lucky this time. They suggested that he start using the elevators at school, but we knew he wouldn't, and surprise, he never did. They told him that since he already had the HIV, now for a couple of years, that he'd probably only have a few more left to live. That's not the kind of thing you tell someone, especially a kid. It's not something that anyone wants to hear, ever, period. However, as much as Jimmy didn't want to hear it, he insisted they tell him truth, and not 'sugar-coat' it at all.

None of us could imagine being Jimmy and having to hear, or even know that you were gonna die while you were still a kid. He was still quick to tell us, despite the knowledge of his fate, that he didn't want any of us to feel sorry for him. And even though us boys, didn't do pity, it was still a tough pill to swallow. He did share something with us, about this whole 'only a few years to live stuff'. He said that he was making a list of all the things that he wanted to do, while he was still alive. It was like a dream list or something, and he seemed pretty serious about it too. He told us that he was gonna keep it in his pocket, every day until he died. Man, was that tough to hear. I mean, knowing that one of your best buds was gonna die was hard enough, but to hear them talk about it was torture. Don't get me wrong, none of us let him know that we felt that way, but it tore at us for sure. The boys were cool. And even though we'd changed over the years, we were still the boys. We had Jimmy's back, and if that meant playing it cool about his disease, then that's what we'd do.

He told us that he was gonna try to do everything on his list, but that we weren't allowed to see it. He also said that he expected us to complete the things that he couldn't, after he was gone. That was when Cindy completely broke down, and didn't stop crying for hours. He said that we didn't have to do them right away, but at some point in our lives we had

to. I think he probably put some stuff on there that he knew

he was never gonna do, just so that we'd have to do them at

some point and that way, we'd always remember him. I

wouldn't be surprised if he put some things on that list that

we wouldn't be able to do until we were adults, on account

that Jimmy did things like that; things you'd never expect.

# Jeremy Aldana

## Jimmy's Old School
## Fall 1992

The reason we all knew so much about the HIV and the AIDS was because we learned them this past year, and not just from Jimmy and Cindy. Our principal was the reason, with the way he went about Jimmy going to our school. Jimmy actually liked our principal, which was almost as weird as our principal being so excited about Jimmy in the first place. See, Jimmy's old school didn't have a good principal, or teachers for that matter, on account that when they found out that Jimmy had the HIV, they all freaked out.

Jimmy told us that, when the school found out about his disease, they all treated him like he was contagious. They looked at him funny, talked about him with weird looks on their faces, and never looked him directly in his eyes. He said that the first week after they told the school, that all of his teachers called in sick. He knew they weren't sick though, and knew how they must've felt about him. He said the kids at school flinched every time he coughed, even if they were on the other side of the room. He said that one time, when he was at lunch and sneezed, every kid bailed out of the cafeteria; every single one. He told us that he cried the whole way home that day.

He told us that they moved here, shortly after that, which makes sense, cause none of us would want to go to a school like that either. We had to convince Jack not to go to Jimmy's old school and beat everyone up. I'm not kidding, Jack really wanted to, but we talked him out of it. You should have seen it. Brad was like one of those hostage negotiators you saw in movies, talking people down off rooftops and talking to the bad guys to get them to release their hostages.

Well, where Jimmy's old school failed, ours succeeded and I think it was because of our principal. At those meetings, with the school board, our principal got it so that we had assemblies about the HIV and the AIDS. He got it so they taught about it in our health class. We even had school-wide fundraisers, where the money collected went to fight the disease, as in finding the cure, and went to scientists so they could research it. The money went to organizations around the country that used it to educated people on the disease, and went to programs that were designed to prevent it.

The whole city embraced the principal's idea, even the students, and everyone learned a lot about the disease. We learned that it was what the doctors called a 'blood-borne' disease, meaning it could only be passed to another person through their blood. That's how Jimmy got it, from a bad transfix, and that's why he wasn't happy when he saw that we became blood-brothers, cause we had cut ourselves and mixed our blood that day. We learned that a person couldn't get it from high-fiving someone who had it, unless you both had bleeding cuts and held on to the high-five for hours. We learned that you couldn't get it from spit, or by hugging. We learned that if someone with the disease coughed or sneezed by you, that you weren't going to get it. We also learned that you couldn't get it from touching doorknobs, or sitting on the same toilet seat as someone with the disease. Most importantly, we learned that we had to learn as much as we could, and then teach others everything we knew.

Stigma is a tough word, it's like stereotype and prejudice. It's what the HIV had clinging to it. It meant that it wasn't the 'norm', and that people who weren't educated about it, got scared and stayed away from it. Dr. Ron told me once that stigmas carried bad things with them, like fear and ignorance. He said that when people were ignorant about things, it was because they were lazy and never took the time to learn about something that they feared, and instead just judged it and ostracized it; never once considering what their actions and words did to those they judged.

People generally feared dying, and it was commonly known, if nothing else was known, that the HIV and the AIDS killed people. So, on some level, I guess I can understand why some people feared the disease, but I still can't figure out why they remained so ignorant about it. Dr.

Ron told me that some people were just plain lazy in their

minds, and thus ignorant, and that some people will always be

that way. We weren't lazy or ignorant, and because of our

principal, not many in our city were.

# BOYS WILL BE BOYS

## Sarah
## Summer 1993

We made it through our sophomore year alright, and Cindy made it through her junior year too. We just had our end of the school year campout last month, and it was a blast, just like always. Even though we were changing; growing up, and things were changing around us, we still had our campouts. We had to buy a bigger tent this year though, on account that we had all gotten bigger. We bought a family size tent, and that seemed to fit all of us good enough, and we liked that it was called 'family-size', cause we were a family; the boys and me.

Cindy was becoming more and more beautiful every day. She let her hair grow out even longer, and it was just plain beautiful. I was now a bit taller, five feet nine inches and weighted right around 200 pounds. It wasn't just me though, all the boys kept growing, even Jimmy. Jack was the only one who seemed to level out, but he was still the biggest kid at school.

Cindy and I 'French-Kissed' this past year, though I still don't know why it's called a French Kiss, just like why fries at McDonald's were called 'French-Fries'; aren't they just kisses and fries? We were taking it slow, on account that we knew we loved each other and that things between us would happen when we were both ready for them to. We were aware of the 'peer pressure', to be sure, but weren't stupid about it. We knew that we didn't have to listen to them to be accepted, on account that we had each other, and we had the boys.

Jack made 'All-State' in football, and went to the finals at state in the 'heavyweight' division of wrestling. He had college scouts at each one of his games and meets, to which he calmly ignored them all. His dad was still in prison, but he stopped calling and stopped writing letters, which made Jack happier. His sister, Sarah, now a teenager, was still in counseling, but told Jack that she didn't want to go anymore. Jack said that she told him she was getting older and wanted to forget everything that their dad did to her. He told us that he understood, cause he wanted to forget too, though we knew he would always remember his 'Louisville Slugger', and the time he spent in Juvenile Hall.

I told him that even though she didn't want to keep going, it was important that she did. I told him that if she quit now, she might start down a path that wouldn't be any good for her. I told him that I still went to Dr. Ron and that I wouldn't be the cool Joey he knows today, if it weren't for me going to see him, despite the fact that I only see him once a month now. If you thought Jack was protective of Jimmy, it didn't come close to how he looked out for his sister.

Jack bought her school clothes, gave her an allowance, and drove her to and from school each day. He went to all of her choir concerts, and parent-teacher conferences too. He was just a big brother raising his sister the best way he knew how. I sometimes wondered if Jack learned a few things from watching Cindy, about how to be a good big sibling. Sarah was never really, officially at least, one of the boys, but this past year she'd been around enough to be thought of as one. She looked up to Cindy, obviously, and Cindy cared just as much for her. They'd play video games together, and Cindy would teach her things that big sisters normally taught their little sisters; stuff like doing their hair and painting their nails.

It was Jimmy, though, that she was most fascinated with. She thought his limp was like the coolest thing since sliced bread, and she learned more about his medicine and disease than any of us did. It was like she was Jimmy's student and I bet she becomes a doctor when she grows up. It was more than that though, on account that Jimmy just knew how to relate to people. He related to us, cause he was our age and liked sports and all the stuff teenage boys did. He related to the kids at school, cause he wasn't afraid to be who he was. He was proud of who he was, disease or no disease! He related to the adults, cause he was so mature for his age and handled everything so well. And he even related to his doctors, who could do nothing but respect his strength and intelligence. He'd smile when he'd tell us about how he'd have a group of doctors around him at the hospital, and how they'd answer all his questions and teach him about what was happening to his body.

He spent most of his time at Jack's this past year, hanging out with him and his sister. Sometimes, Cindy would go with him, but most of the time she stayed with me. Jimmy, Jack, and Sarah would tell us all about the things they did over there. Most of the time, they played Monopoly though, to which Jimmy told us that he'd sometimes let Sarah win. Oh boy did we all give him crap when we heard that, on account that it was Jimmy who always insisted that we never treat him that way. Now, we find out that he was doing the same thing he refused to let us do! We planned on letting him have it, despite the fact that we understood and were actually glad that he cared that much about her. When we called him on it, he said, "I don't let her win all the time!"

Jack's mom stopped going to the mental hospital every week, and was taking her meds on her own. She was trying to be a mom, and Jack said that she doesn't walk around like a zombie anymore. He says that she still doesn't work, but is getting a disability check from the state every month to cover some of the household bills. Overall, we were happy for Jack and Sarah, because they were surviving. However, I couldn't help but think that if Jimmy hadn't spent so much time there, that they would've fallen apart instead of growing closer together.

Somehow, Jimmy seemed to have that effect on people. I'm not sure if it's a gift; wait, I know it's a gift, but I'm just not sure if he had it cause he was dying or if he'd had it all of his life.

# BOYS WILL BE BOYS

## Jobs
## Summer 1993

Just like Jack had a job, he worked at a neighborhood auto repair shop, we all had jobs. Cindy and I both worked at the movie theater on Greenfield Avenue, working on the weekends, and on some weeknights when people called in sick. It was tough, in the beginning, going back there with all the history it held for me, but Cindy helped me through it, holding my hand every day that we went into work. Literally, we held hands in the car on the way over and then all the way into the theater. I usually drove, on account that I always wanted to and she never had a problem with that.

I got Jake's car after he was gone, and Jack always fixed it for free, even though I tried to pay him every time. He'd always tell me that it wasn't going to happen, 'no way-no how'. However, I managed to 'one-up' him, cause I always let him and Sarah get into the movies for free. It was an understood arrangement by both parties involved, namely me and him. Whenever the boys pitched a fit, cause I made them pay for their movies, I simply asked them if they fixed my car when it broke down. They all just shook their heads and emptied their wallets.

Brad and Paul both worked at the pizza place in the strip mall, made decent dough (get it), and occasionally, brought pizzas back for us when they got off work. We spent most weekends at my house, hanging out in my little apartment, in the basement. Seeing as how there was only one bed, Cindy and I got that, and Jimmy got the loveseat. The rest of the boys all camped out in their sleeping bags on the floor.

Andy started smoking this past year, so we made him sleep under the window, which was cracked open, on account that his clothes reeked of cigarette smoke. Cindy and I offered up our bed one weekend to him, with the only condition being that he not smoke for two whole days. He couldn't do it, so he slept under the window as usual. And of course, we made him go outside to smoke. We tried telling

him to quit, but it was no use. He was gonna do it anyway, no

matter what we told him. He said, "Heck my folks don't care

if I smoke, so why do you guys?"

He worked at the grocery store, bagging groceries. He

told us that his boss was gonna teach him the register once

school started, to which he seemed pleased enough about.

We all talked one day, and decided that it would be best if

someone went outside with him when he smoked at my

house, to keep him company. It wasn't because we thought it

was okay to smoke, but because we knew how he'd feel if we

allowed him to be an outcast among us. Remember, we were

the boys, and that meant sticking together, no matter what,

and if that meant hanging out with Andy while he smoked,

then so be it.

None of us smoked again, after we tried it at Andy's

insistence, probably cause we couldn't breathe right for like

the next two hours or so. He knew how we felt about it, and

would simply ask us if we wanted to come hang out for a few minutes. Sometimes we all went out with him, but most of the time just a few of us did. He never asked Jimmy to come, cause he knew that 'second-hand smoke' probably wasn't what Jimmy needed most, but that never stopped Jimmy, cause he went outside with Andy almost every time.

We figured that Andy started smoking to get his parents attention or at least a reaction from them, but it had the exact opposite effect, cause his parents never told him not to smoke and actually always kept a carton of smokes in the fridge for him. We didn't know if his parents were making an affectionate gesture to him, as in supporting something he did, or if they were helping him kill himself. He said they didn't smoke, so we knew the smokes were for him. We still worry about him though, on account that his parents still have never told him that they loved him. And I swear he'd be better off living with me and my aunt and uncle, but every time I suggest it to him, he tells me 'no'.

# BOYS WILL BE BOYS

Jimmy had a job as a paper delivery boy for our local paper, which he was good at, though it made him tired from all the walking and lifting he did. We all pitched in and bought him a wagon to pull his papers around in, to which he reluctantly accepted. He didn't like pity, but knew that he'd never make money if he didn't have a wagon to ease the pain from carrying all those papers every day. His paper route was huge; over a mile in total distance, but the wagon was only used a few times.

Jimmy could drive, and we offered up our cars for him to use on his route, but he told us no. He even made a joke of telling us no, and did it without making us feel bad. I'm telling you, Jimmy had a way about himself, which made him one cool kid. He told Jack that he didn't want to use his truck, cause Jack needed it to pick up Sarah every day. He told Brad and Paul that he didn't want to use their car, the one they 'co-owned' as they called it, cause they needed it more, on account that both of them used it and he didn't want to burden them. He told Cindy and me that he didn't want to get 'in the way of our love' by taking away our 'vehicle of romance', to which he got socked in the arm by me and kicked in his good leg by her. He told Andy that he couldn't deliver the papers on the 'green limousine', by which he meant the city transit bus, cause Andy only rode the bus and refused to own a car.

He did say that if he was gonna 'cheat' and use a car for his route, it would only be with Mark's car. For some reason he refused to drive, which was weird to all of us, on account that he just got his driver's license. Maybe he didn't want to drive, cause he knew he'd like it so much and since he knew he'd die soon, he didn't want to get attached to it only to have to get it up. Even still, I had a tough time understanding that one, on account that a kid getting his license was a rite of passage into another realm of freedom. I guess I really didn't need to know why he didn't want to drive. I let it go, knowing that he must've had a good reason.

# BOYS WILL BE BOYS

Mark still had a tough time getting along with people, just as he always had, even though we could never figure out exactly why. He'd had two different jobs this past year, but quit them both after getting into big arguments with his managers. He worked at Denny's as a dishwasher and then at Brad and Paul's pizza place, as a delivery driver. Despite his bouncing around, he still managed to make his car payments and insurance payments, and even managed to put a little bit away into his savings.

None of us were all that surprised when Jimmy offered to split his money with Mark, if he drove him around and helped him with his route. He told Mark that with his car, they could take a bigger route and make more money. Jimmy had one condition though, that Mark took the job as seriously as he did. He said that Mark had to show up on time every day and not be 'grubbed out'. He said that Mark had to dress like he would for any other job, show up with a good attitude, tone down his anger, and do most of the talking when they collected.

Collecting money was the toughest part of the paper route, though it did have its rewards. The rewards were the tips you got sometimes, but the tough part was asking people to pay their bills. Mark and Jimmy told us that they heard 'every excuse in the book'. They managed alright, I guess, and even nabbed us a paper every day. Their partnership actually worked out pretty good. They made a bunch of money, laughed a lot, and Mark was finally able to keep a job where he didn't fight with his boss.

# BOYS WILL BE BOYS

## Mary
## Fall 1993

Mary ran away from Brad and his family a little more than three years ago, and nobody heard from her until this past year. I'll admit it was weird, at first, but it made sense when I got a letter from her. In the letter, was a sealed envelope addressed to Brad, and a letter to me. She told me that she was sorry about my family, but was glad that I had the boys there for me. She asked how school was going, and how the boys were doing. She even thanked me for always being there for her 'baby brother'. Her letter made me smile.

In her letter, she asked me to give Brad the envelope and have him write a letter back to her. She didn't put her address on Brad's envelope, she explained in my letter, cause she didn't want her parents knowing where she was. The return address said that she was living in Seattle, Washington, a couple thousand miles from us. I did as she asked, and gave Brad her letter.

Brad, who was normally composed, smiled from ear to ear and let out what I could only describe as a yelp. Immediately, he noticed that there was no return address and I answered his puzzled look by telling him Mary's plan. He was so excited that he grabbed Andy and told him to go outside with him, while he read his letter. I couldn't really explain how Brad felt, but I can tell you that I've never seen him that excited before. He left my room so fast, that he would've made 'Speedy Gonzales' and the 'Road Runner' proud.

He didn't let us see the letter when we all asked him about it later. He said he would, but not right then, and we left it at that. After all, look at me with this journal; of course, I could understand. He did tell us about it though, and asked if he could see my letter and envelope. I let him, but told him to make sure that he left it at my house, on account that Mary didn't want their parents to know where she was. She was an adult now, and her parents couldn't make her come home or do anything else for that matter. See, in this great country of ours, the great 'U S of A', once a kid turns 18 years old, then their parents no longer had control over them. Brad told us that Mary just wasn't ready to talk to their parents yet, and asked that he not tell them. He kinda laughed at that, cause he almost never saw his dad, who was always on the road, and he barely ever saw his mom.

Brad said her letter was short, but that she promised to make the next one longer. He said she had a big apartment, just outside the city, and a good job at a hospital as a nurse's assistant. He told us that she didn't do drugs anymore and was having a great time. The only other thing she said, he told us, was that it had been rough when she first got out there, but the tough times only made her stronger.

It wasn't long before he handed me his letter to her, so I could send it off. I sent it off, but had to put a few extra stamps on it, on account that it was so heavy. He had written something like ten pages, which I guess made sense, cause he hadn't talked to her in so long.

They wrote back and forth for months, before he dropped the 'bombshell' on us. Mary had written her parents a letter, and hadn't sent anymore to my house, since the first one. We never gave a second thought to Brad doing all kinds of research on Seattle, cause we just figured he was showing an interest in where his sister lived. We didn't even think anything of it when, for 'Spring Break', he and Paul flew to Seattle to visit Mary. We actually thought it was cool that they were flying on an airplane; going to one of the coolest cities and most beautiful states in the country, and that Brad was finally gonna get to see his sister, who he missed so much.

We all pretty much reacted the same way, when Brad and Paul told us that they were moving to Seattle to live with Mary (that was the bombshell). I mean, don't get me wrong, we were glad that they were gonna get to go live in Seattle, but man, none of us boys had ever left before, and we weren't necessarily ready for them to leave. We were torn

between always being there for each other, no matter what

(which now meant supporting their move to Seattle), and not

wanting to break up the boys. We knew that by supporting

them in their move that we were being there for them, just

like we always promised we would. And even though, we

knew that someday (just like Brad's dad told us all those years

ago) we'd all go our separate ways, we never thought it would

happen before we finished high school.

We were all in a weird kinda daze for a while, after

they first told us about their plan to move. We weren't

surprised that Paul was going with Brad, cause over the last

few years, they were pretty much inseparable. Paul's parents

weren't as easily convinced as we were, or as Brad's were.

Brad's parents figured that if Mary was strong enough and

smart enough to make it in the world, when she left, then

chances were that Brad was too. He was mature and

responsible; always had been, since any of us could

remember, and I guess his parents could see that. Paul, on the

other hand, had grown up pretty much with us, and his

parents hadn't really noticed all the changes that we had.

They were more scared for him than anything, but after they

talked to Mary, who flew back to get them, they ended up

allowing Paul go.

Individually, we each had our own thoughts on their

big move. Cindy was stoked to meet Mary, and was super

happy for Brad and Paul. She told them that they better have

a place for us to visit in a few years, to which they eagerly

agreed. Jack was cool with it, though he more or less just

nodded or grunted whenever the topic of them moving came

up. Brad and Paul were moving up in the world. They were

heading out on their own and would make it just fine, I

thought. They were both bright; Brad, always the peacemaker,

and Paul the comedian. They would show Seattle what us

boys were made of!

# BOYS WILL BE BOYS

Mark was excited for them, but didn't talk much about it. Andy kinda didn't seem to care, but we knew he did. His parents were still doing a number on him, and I kinda think that he might've either been upset or jealous about it, maybe both. He didn't grunt like Jack or anything, but I noticed he stopped looking at Brad and Paul when he talked to them. He was always doing something when he talked with them, so he could still turn away if he felt he needed to. I think he might've been jealous of them, cause Mary had cared enough about Brad to come back for him. And I think he might've been upset with them too, on account that they were getting an opportunity to start over somewhere new.

Jimmy was cool with it, telling us all how brave Brad and Paul were. And if there was anyone who could talk about bravery, it was Jimmy. He was right, too, cause what they were doing took guts. As for me, well I was happy for them, and was sad for me and the boys. And though I knew that we were only losing them to Mary and Seattle, and not for good,

I couldn't help but feel like we were losing them forever. I made them agree to call and write and stuff, but other than that, I'd made the decision to let them do their thing.

It was sad when friends moved away, went to new towns with new schools, and made new friends. Brad and Paul were part of the boys, and were there from the beginning. They were family, and they were leaving, and that hurt. We were all sad to see them go, but we knew they'd be okay. Mary had a room for them, and they had enough money in their savings to last them a while, so we all knew they'd be alright. After all, they were part of the boys, and remember, us boys knew how to survive. We knew how to take care of each other, and knew more than the world ever gave us credit for. Yea, they're gonna make it just fine, both of them, together.

## Alone
## Fall 1994

I've noticed that as I get older, more time elapses between my writings. I was thinking that maybe it was cause I was becoming closer to being a man, and that I could hold my emotions in longer. I'm not sure exactly why I write when I do, but I know that I must be doing it for some reason. Cindy says she likes that I write; she likes my poems to her, my essays, and my stories. I even shared with her my dream of being a writer someday.

I stopped seeing Dr. Ron this past year. In fact, I haven't seen him since last winter. I'd been so accustom to seeing him every week, then every month, and then whenever I needed to talk, that I thought I'd never stop going to see him. However, I was apparently wrong, cause as soon as I got to his office, he shook my hand, gave me my file folder, and told me that I didn't have to see him anymore. After I left his office that day, I was feeling all sorts of strange emotions;

ones I hadn't felt in a long time. I sorta felt all alone, you know, like I was being abandoned. It wasn't just him though, cause those feelings were coming from everywhere, and from everyone.

After Brad and Paul moved, they called a few times and wrote only once. Even then, the letter was more like a note. Yea, I know, 'Boo-Hoo', right. I was acting like a big baby. Well, that's how I talked it out with Cindy, anyway. She told me that I wasn't being a baby, that she and the rest of the boys all missed them too. She told me that I shouldn't trip just then, on account that they still were adjusting to their new lives, and it wasn't all that uncommon for teenage boys to not write letters, and I guess she was right. She also told me that Dr. Ron was letting me go, cause he knew that I was ready to and that I should look at it like that instead of looking at it like I was being abandoned.

It wasn't just Brad and Paul leaving though, Jimmy had gotten real sick just before school and it threw us all out of whack. We thought he had just gotten a cold or something, but his fever was real high one day, like 103 Degrees Fahrenheit and his folks took him to the hospital. He was in there for a week and the doctors were telling him that his white blood cell count was his lowest yet. We all brought '7-UP' and 'Saltines' each day, hung out with him, and at least one of us stayed each night on the cot one of the nurses brought us.

Jack, Sarah, and their mom had been getting along better than ever before, and while that was great, we got to see less of them. I know, selfish right? Mark had taken over the route mainly by himself, since Jimmy got sick. Which, I guess was good for Mark, responsibility and all, but that meant that he was around less also. Andy had completely gone off the radar after Jimmy got out of the hospital, and we were lucky if we saw him once a week. Cindy turned down the honor of being our 'Homecoming Queen', cause she wanted to be available if Jimmy got sick again. She was beautiful and sweeter than you could ever imagine, but even I felt her pull away from time to time.

When she graduated, she almost seemed not to care about what a great job she did in finishing high school. Jimmy was the only one, it seemed, who hadn't gone anywhere, but even he was dying. I know that no one was abandoning me; it was just that I hadn't felt that way since mom, Jake, and Bobby died, and I wasn't sure what I was supposed to do with those feelings.

After their accident, I had Dr. Ron and the boys there for me, each and every step of the way, but now it seemed like they were all gone, even though I knew better. I knew that he was right in letting me go, on account that I was 17 years old now, a senior in high school, and growing into a man. I had a beautiful and wonderful girlfriend, a job, a car, and the best set of friends anywhere. Life was still okay for me, but I did hit a few rough spots every now and then.

# BOYS WILL BE BOYS

## Skipping School
## Winter 1994

This past fall, I think, was the toughest yet for me, and I guess it showed that I was growing up. And as tough as it was for me, it was worse for Andy. It was our first day back at school, as seniors, when Mark and Jimmy found him in his bathroom. They went over to check on him, when he didn't show up for school. When they got to his house, his parent's cars were gone and they parked in the driveway. They said they knocked a bunch of times, and then went inside on their own, when Andy didn't answer the door.

Andy was at home most of the time, and if he wasn't, he was either at work, school, or at my house. Mark and Jimmy said they talked to him a few days before, made plans to go out that night, and were supposed to pick him up after school. They didn't really care why he skipped school; they just wanted to make sure he was okay. We were all worried about him, on account that he was more depressed lately than he'd ever been before. They said that when they got inside, they saw his shoes by the front door, called for him, and when he didn't answer back, they went upstairs to his room. Mark made it up to Andy's room first, on account that Jimmy's legs were getting worse and he now had a 'walking stick' to deal with. They met at the top of the stairs, where Mark told him that Andy wasn't in his bedroom.

Jimmy said he saw a light under the hallway bathroom door, looked at Mark, and then went down the hall. The door was closed, but not locked, and they said they feared the worst. When they pushed the door open, they saw Andy slumped in the bathtub, like he had passed out from a hard night of drinking. Jimmy said he saw Andy's eyes first, and Mark said he saw the blood first. Jimmy said that Andy's eyes looked like they were smiling, even though his mouth showed no smile or frown, as weird as that sounds. He swore that Andy's eyes were smiling, and that he almost seemed at peace. Mark saw something different, altogether, and said that when he saw the pool of blood in the bathtub, he saw the opposite of peace. He saw the 'up-and-down' cuts on Andy's arms, and the blood that ran down into the drain. He said he couldn't even look at Andy's face right away.

Jimmy had to snap his fingers to get Mark's attention, to have him go back to Andy's room and call 911. Mark came back with Andy's cordless phone, as Jimmy was checking Andy's neck for a pulse. Mark had to give the phone to Jimmy, cause he was in shock at seeing Andy lying there in the bathtub. Jimmy called 911, and then he called me. After he called and told Cindy and me about what happened, I called Jack at work and told him to meet us at Andy's. It surprised Cindy and me, but not Jack that all three of us made it to Andy's before the ambulance did. We got there just before Jack, and I asked Cindy to go up and make sure that Jimmy and Mark were okay. I waited for Jack, on account that I didn't tell him over the phone about Andy killing himself, cause I knew he was gonna flip out. He was gonna be pissed, so I knew I had to wait and tell him face-to-face.

When Jack got there, he wanted to run into the house. When I held him back at the front door, I saw the look in his eyes and knew that he must've figured it out. I could only hold him back for a minute, and luckily Mark came down the stairs and helped me get Jack to sit down on the front steps. He was crying and Mark was fighting to hold his tears back, when I suggested that it would be best if he and I didn't go inside. Jimmy and Cindy stayed upstairs until the paramedics got there and brought Andy down with them. When me and Jack saw Andy on that gurney, even with the white sheet pulled over him, we stopped talking and just followed him and the medics as they got inside the ambulance.

Cindy, Jimmy, Mark, Jack, and me waited there, on Andy's front steps, until his folks got home from their jobs. We all talked, after they took Andy away, and decided that if

# BOYS WILL BE BOYS

Andy's folks hadn't cared enough about him to prevent this, then we weren't going to care enough about them to call and tell them. Jack and Jimmy had gone back inside, after Andy was gone and before his folks got home, and got some things from Andy's room. Jack told Jimmy where to find Andy's secret shoe box, with all of his most important possessions, while he went to Andy's closet and got Andy's old pair of sneakers. Mark and me both looked at the sneakers, as they came out with Jack and Jimmy, then we looked at Jack and started laughing our butts off. The sneakers Jack were holding were Andy's old pair of ProWings, back from when Jack was younger and more rebellious. Andy used to tell us that he'd kept them over the years, but none of us believed him until now, though Jack must've had some idea that Andy had been telling the truth.

The laugh we had went away as quickly as it came, when Andy's folks pulled their cars in front of their house. We didn't have to tell them what happened, cause their neighbors did that for us, the second they got out of their cars. Andy's mom started crying and they actually looked like real tears, but his dad looked right past her, at us. His dad yelled something at us, from the curb, and starting running towards Jimmy. We all stepped in front of Jimmy, just before Andy's dad reached him. He had his arms out, in front of him, and was trying to grab Andy's box out of Jimmy's hands, while Andy's mom just wept on the hood of her car. Andy's dad kept yelling at us to give him back his son's things, something about stealing from private property, when his eyes told us that he'd gone too far.

Andy's dad saw Jack coming, but froze like them deer in those headlights did, and couldn't react in time to save himself. Jack came from behind Jimmy, who was behind Mark, Cindy, and me, and I didn't even notice Jack going past us until I saw Andy's dad and his deer eyes. None of us tried to hold Jack back, not even a little, on account that he was hitting him for all of us, including Andy. It only took one punch, and I'm surprised that after Andy's dad went flying

into the air and then onto his back, that Jack hadn't gotten on

top of him and beaten him good. Jack could've too, cause

none of us would've moved a muscle to stop him.

We all took in the blood that covered Andy's dad's

face, probably from a broken nose, while Jack bent down and

said a few choice words to him. In his loudest voice, Jack told

everyone in the neighborhood what a terrible father Andy's

dad was. Jack also told him that Andy's box was now ours,

and that Andy was more a part of our family than he ever was

theirs. He ended his yelling by shouting, "If you'd just loved

him, like we had, then he wouldn't have killed himself!"

When Jack was finished, we grabbed Andy's ProWings and

shoebox, and left. After we were gone, we promised we'd

never go back.

# Jeremy Aldana

## Giving Back
## Winter 1994

We called Brad and Paul, told them about Andy, and they flew back for his funeral. Andy died on a Tuesday and his funeral was on Saturday, at the local church. It was an open casket viewing, which meant that we were able to see our bud and say goodbye, one last time. Andy's dad had a massive bruise on his nose and two blackened eyes, from where Jack had laid him out.

Cindy had already graduated, but Mark, Jimmy, and me wrote notes for ourselves to get out of school for the week. The principal was cool about it, on account that he knew Andy from when he first worked with us on the fundraisers after Jimmy came to our school. He told us to take as much time as we needed, to which we all told him 'thanks'. We took our notes into the school at Brad and Paul's request, cause they needed to visit it for some reason. Andy's locker had already been emptied, by us, but it had also been decorated by the kids at school, which was way cool, on account that we knew that he would've been pleased with that.

On Saturday, we all walked to the church, each of us wearing our nicest slacks, shirts, and ties. Cindy said that we all looked 'handsome', but none of us knew if we should accept a compliment on the day of our bud's funeral. She told us that we were being foolish, cause Andy was in there, even in his casket, dressed all nice and at the very least, we owed it to him to look our best as well. We decided not to go to the burial, but to stay for the eulogy and the viewing, and then leave. It was a 'packed house'; an audience Andy would've approved of, and Brad gave just about the best eulogy that was ever given. He didn't get mushy or nothing, instead just told everyone how good of a friend Andy was, how smart he was, and how he was one of 'the boys'.

We had decided, as a group, before the funeral, that it would've been important to Andy that we bury something with him. It was weird, you know, how Andy's shoe box, when we opened it, had only six pieces of paper in it. With Jack giving Andy his ProWings back, that left the rest of us with one sheet of paper each. When it was time, we all walked up to Andy, said goodbye to him, and gave him back his most prized possessions.

Mark started and gave Andy back his 6th grade report card, placing it next to him. Brad went next, giving him back his 'ACT' score of '34', placing it next to Mark's gift. Paul went next, giving him back his 'SAT' score of '2100'. Then I went, and gave him back his last letter from the principal, that congratulated him on his honor roll placement for the fourth year in a row, with a cumulative 'GPA' of '4.0'. Cindy went after me, and gave him back his college acceptance letter from the 'University of Wisconsin'. Jack went after her, giving him back his pair of ProWings. Jimmy went last, which I guess was kinda fitting, on account that he had the most important piece of the whole group.

# BOYS WILL BE BOYS

We all came back up to Andy and Jimmy, held hands with each other, and watched as Jimmy gave Andy back the set of rules we made up for initiating Cindy and Jimmy into the boys. You know, I always wondered where those rules went. And as we all said goodbye to our bud for the last time, I looked at his face and knew Jimmy was right. Andy was peaceful now.

# Jeremy Aldana

## Good News-Bad News
## Fall 1995

So much has happened to us in the last few years, that I think we all could've lived a couple of lifetimes. Some good news, but then more bad news, and then some more good news, but then some more bad news. Yea, that's how it's been for us, one roller coaster ride after another. We wanted to celebrate Andy's life and had decided, that every year on his birthday we'd all come back to La Follette Park for a game of '500' in his honor. We were adults now, but we were still 'The Boys', and that meant we kept our word, no matter what! And, guess what? Brad and Paul came out, from Seattle, like they promised they would, and we all went to La Follette Park and played just one game of '500' for Andy.

With me, it's the good news first, if it's possible. And so with that said, this past summer I proposed to Cindy and she said yes! She was going to the local community college, and she was going to be my bride. She and Jimmy moved in with me, and my aunt and uncle moved out. They told me, once I graduated, that they were going to move back to their old house. They told me that mom had almost paid off the house, before she passed away, and they pitched in a little to finish off the payments. I accepted the offer to take the house over completely, with a hug from my aunt and a firm handshake from my uncle. It didn't take Cindy and I long to move from the basement to the upstairs. And it sure wasn't much longer after that, when she announced that she wanted to paint and redecorate. I had no problem with any of that, as long as it made her happy. Jimmy took my old room; Jake's old room, in the basement, and didn't change a thing.

Remember when I said that whole thing about good news first, well then that means that there is some bad news down the line and since I already wrote about Cindy and me, now I have to write about what wasn't so good.

When Brad and Paul were getting ready to leave, while we were all at mine and Cindy's house celebrating our engagement, they asked that we not call them back home unless the news was good. We all laughed, told them 'sure thing', and then as we were saying our goodbyes, Jimmy collapsed into the coffee table, smashing the glass in the middle. We didn't care about the engagement anymore, on account that we knew Jimmy was more important. We just wanted him to be okay. He made it farther than any doctor, or scientist, said he would. He showed them all, and did it with a smile on his face. He'd given speeches to the community and to charities, raising money for HIV/AIDS awareness, research, prevention, and a cure. He'd write letters to other kids, who got the disease and was their lifeline by retelling his survival story to them, so they'd hold on to hope themselves. There's no counting how many lives he must've saved.

After he fell, we rushed him to the ER and told them what happened. We told them about his disease, and Cindy remembered to bring his medication. She called their parents, who rushed down to the hospital and met us outside the ER. The doctors told the nurses to have us wait in the lobby, which is where we waited until they came and got us. The ER doctor told us that they were moving him upstairs into a more comfortable room, to which the doctor received a bunch of dropped jaws and blank stares. He politely told us that he would meet us upstairs, gave us the room number, and told us that if we wanted to go home and get some of Jimmy's personal belongings, then that would be fine.

We all just kinda stood there, in the ER lobby, with these 'dumbfounded' looks on our faces, looking at each other to see if anyone had any idea what the doctor was talking about. Jimmy's parents were the first to ask why he was getting a room upstairs, if he just fell through the coffee table glass. It wasn't that it was a minor injury or anything, but they just figured it required an overnight stay at the most, even with his HIV. Jack spoke next, addressing all of us, though not looking any of us in our eyes, and told us why

Jimmy was staying in the hospital overnight and maybe longer. He said that Jimmy had been going to his appointments by himself this past year, and that he wasn't completely honest with us all. He said that Jimmy swore him to secrecy, but had a backdoor plan for Jack, in case just this sorta thing happened, and then he wanted Jack to tell everybody instead of the doctors doing it.

Jack, still looking at his big feet, told us that Jimmy had contracted AIDS some time ago, and had been slowly dying. Jimmy's mom then collapsed into her husband's arms, sobbing into his shoulder. Cindy was in my arms, and crying on my shoulder as well, when Jack said that he, Mark, Brad, and Paul were gonna go and get some of Jimmy's things and come right back.

The boys met us back at Jimmy's room, with his things in a small plastic bag. Jack showed us, when we met him in the hallway, what was in the bag. There were only envelopes in the bag and I got a small sense of 'déjà vu', on account that there were exactly six of them. Jack only showed us, but told us that Jimmy had given him specific instructions concerning the letters. He told us that he intended to honor Jimmy's wishes, and we nodded and stepped aside to let him through.

Jimmy was asleep when we saw him that first night, but was awake the next day. None of us left his room, which really made the room slash suite, the hospital provided for us, more of a necessity than a luxury. The doctors told us that Jimmy had developed a tumor, and that the cancer had moved so fast, destroying what little defenses he still had, that he had only a very short time left.

When we saw Jimmy, he told us to 'knock off' all the 'crying and junk', saying something about us all knowing that this day would come. That was before the big coughing fit, and before we had to step out of the room so the doctors and nurses could attend to him. When he sent the nurses for us, we came back with his envelopes and Jack gave them back to him. Jimmy said that he was tired, and that he was ready to go. He told us that he loved us all, and that we had to take care of each other and never forget what we've been through. He told us that we were the reason he fought so hard to live, that we were the ones he lived for.

He gave us each our own envelopes, with his parents and Brad and Paul being the exceptions, cause theirs were addressed to both parents and to both Brad and Paul. He shook each of our hands, as firm as he could, as he gave us our letters. It was almost like he was presenting us with awards, if that was possible. He even put Jack on his knees with the squeeze he put on, though I think Jack let him have that one.

Jimmy caught himself before another coughing fit and told his mom and dad that he loved them very much, and he thanked them for never giving up on him. He then turned to Cindy and said the three most precious words she'd ever heard, and never dreamed she would, "I forgive you."

# BOYS WILL BE BOYS

Cindy broke down, but held onto me tight, and I know she did it for her little brother, who just released all of her burdens from her shoulders, giving her the gift she needed most. He then told us that he ripped up his 'list', on account that he had everything he ever wanted and needed in his room, at that moment. Then, out of left field, for him anyway, he asked us all for a group hug. He had never asked any of us for a hug before, not even his parents, who had to steal them when he wasn't looking.

We all looked at each other, without saying a word, then at Jimmy, and went in for a hug. We all squeezed, letting our love pour over him, and as we pulled back, we saw his eyes close and blink out a tear and knew that he was gone.

# Jeremy Aldana

## Boys Will Be Boys
## Fall 2000

It's been five years since Jimmy's passing, and I thought it was a good time for my last entry. Cindy and I got married in the summer of 1999, amid the world's scare of Y2K, on account that we knew better than to be scared of some date, and because we weren't too worried about the world falling apart.

Every year on Andy's birthday, we still get together for our game at La Follette Park, where the only thing that changed was that we played two games instead of just one. We played the first game for Andy, and the second for Jimmy.

Even though we were all part of 'The Boys', and one family, we all decided to keep our letters from Jimmy private, agreeing that they were between us and him.

Brad and Paul still live in Seattle and work for some big computer company. Lots of 'high-tech' stuff, they said.

# BOYS WILL BE BOYS

Jack decided not to go 'pro', and he and his sister, Sarah, opened up a counseling center for 'troubled and abused teens'.

Mark kept delivering papers and now manages the local delivery routes, always giving jobs to high school kids.

Cindy married me, went into nursing, and now works with her parents at their foundation for HIV/AIDS awareness, named after Jimmy.

As for me, well, I became the luckiest guy on Earth when Cindy said yes to being my wife, and since then I've decided to follow my dream of being a writer. And even though I haven't seen Dr. Ron in years, something he said to me years ago, pretty much sums up my life...

"Boys Will Be Boys."

Jeremy Aldana

**The End**

Made in the USA
Charleston, SC
21 December 2013